Utterly yours, Booker Jones

by Betsy Duffey

PUFFIN BOOKS

PUFFIN BOOKS

Published by the Penguin Group

Penguin Putnam Inc., 375 Hudson Street, New York, New York 10014, U.S.A.

Penguin Books Ltd, 27 Wrights Lane, London W8 5TZ, England

Penguin Books Australia Ltd, Ringwood, Victoria, Australia

Penguin Books Canada Ltd, 10 Alcorn Avenue, Toronto, Ontario, Canada M4V 3B2

Penguin Books (N.Z.) Ltd, 182-190 Wairau Road, Auckland 10, New Zealand

Penguin Books Ltd, Registered Offices: Harmondsworth, Middlesex, England

First published in the United States of America by Viking,
a division of Penguin Books USA Inc., 1995
Published in Puffin Books, 1997

7 9 10 8

THE LIBRARY OF CONGRESS HAS CATALOGED THE VIKING EDITION AS FOLLOWS:

Duffey, Betsy.

Utterly yours, Booker Jones / by Betsy Duffey. p. cm. "Ages 10 up".
Summary: Middle school student and aspiring author Booker Jones is
evicted from his bedroom when his grandfather moves in, creating
problems both at home and at school.
ISBN 0-670-86007-7
[1. Authorship—Fiction. 2. Grandfathers—Fiction. 3. Middle school—Fiction.
4. Schools—Fiction. 5. Family life—Fiction.] I. Title.
PZ7.D876Ut 1995 [Fic]—dc20 95-11143 CIP AC

Puffin Books ISBN 0-14-037496-5

Printed in the United States of America

For Amy

Contents

Utterly yours,
Booker Jones

Booker Jones
Pickle Springs, AR

March 4

Hamerstein Books
New York, NY

Dear Editor,

Here is my latest book, WORMS FROM THE
PLANET SPAGHETTI, the best book in the history
of the United States. When it becomes a movie,
I want to play the part of Captain Dirtex. Some
of the kids in my school might think that I
should be one of the worms. Ha! What do they
know?

In the beginning, the spaceship is traveling through darkest space. In the distance
they see a new planet.

"I don't see that planet on the map,
Captain!"

"Check again, First Mate."

"Wow, Captain. I think you had better
take a look at this!"

As they fly closer, they realize that the
entire planet is actually a giant ball of
spaghetti. As they watch, one giant tentacle
begins to unwind and reach for the spaceship!
But . . . I don't want to spoil it for you!

Hopefully yours,

Booker Jones
Author-to-be

Booker Jones
Pickle Springs, AR

March 16

Hamerstein Books
New York, NY

Dear Editor:

Enclosed is my new book, MOON MUMMY, the
best book in the history of the world. You will
love it, I'm sure.

It starts as man first lands on the moon.
One small step for man, one giant step for mummy!
(That's just a little inside joke. You will see
how funny it really is when you read the book!)

The astronauts bounce out in their space
suits and notice a large crater. One turns to
the other.

"It's so quiet," he says.

"Too quiet," the other one answers.

From deep inside the crater they notice a
small movement . . .

Read it to find out what happens!

Optimistically yours,

Booker Jones
Your favorite writer?

1

Crash Landing

Booker pulled the white sheet of typing paper out of the typewriter with a snap and held it up to admire. His round face glowed with creative energy; his glasses twinkled in the light of his reading lamp under the dining room table.

```
SPACE COWS
    by
Booker Jones
```

It was perfection. The best title in the history of Pickle Springs, Arkansas. No, the United States. No, the world. No, the universe!

He loved typing title pages more than anything. It was always a moment of great hope. The start of a brand-new book and a brand-new future as a novelist.

Booker pulled two pieces of tape off a plastic roll, folded them, and stuck them to the back of the page. Then he crawled out from under the table to press the page up on the wall with his other title pages, right between *Worms from the Planet Spaghetti* and *Moon Mummy.* Twenty-three title pages now papered the dining room wall.

The table was covered with two large flowered sheets. They draped down around it, forming a tent. Booker's new bedroom. It had been his bedroom for only four weeks, but he had already started two novels in it.

The rest of the dining room was filled with his grandfather's things: Pop's musty boxes filled with old newspapers and cameras, fishing poles and boots. On top of the boxes were piles of clothes on hangers and a large black-and-white picture of some kind of fish staring out from a dusty frame.

Two plants, shriveled now, stood in the corners of the room, their brown leaves littering the floor, the dirt balls hard and dry inside their pots.

Booker ignored the boxes and plants as he crawled back under the table and pulled the sheet into place. He adjusted the clip-on light and rolled in another white piece of typing paper. He licked his lips and pushed his glasses up, then stretched his fingers and smoothed down his cowlick. The typewriter hummed in the silence, and his fingers trembled a little above the keys.

He liked to start his books with action. He closed his eyes, and suddenly he was there on the cowship with the space cows. He began to type.

Chapter One

A-MOO-GA!

A-MOO-GA!

Warning lights flashed on the cowship. Warning signals sounded the alert. The ship blasted through darkest space at warp speed, out of control. Out of control and headed for a crash landing.

A-MOO-GA! THIRTY SECONDS TO IMPACT!

The voice of the ship's computer counted off the seconds. The seconds left until the crash.

Calmly and professionally the space cows prepared for a crash landing. They had practiced the drill many times before in preparation for possible disaster. Now the disaster had come.

He reached the bottom of the page and pulled the paper out of the typewriter. Quickly, his mind still on the cowship, he rolled another sheet into place. He peeked outside the tent. No sign of his mother.

His mother hardly ever glanced into the dining room anymore as she hurried by with trays and medicine for Pop. Maybe it made her remember the time when the dining room had been perfect. The table had been a gleaming expanse of red wood, glowing, with a vase of fresh flowers in the center on a rectangular mirror.

He remembered that time, too. He used to polish the table for his mother with a spray bottle of lemon-smelling polish. He would rub until his reflection gleamed back at him from the wood. The table had not been polished in a long time.

And the plants had been palms. They had been green. His mother used to water them with a watering can and clip the dead leaves with silver scissors.

At least things were perfect under the table. Booker's sleeping bag was rolled out in the middle. On each side of the sleeping bag were boxes of his things— organized and neat, not like the odd collection of things against the wall.

He sat on the sleeping bag cross-legged in front of an old electric typewriter.

This was the one good thing that had come from Pop's moving in. The typewriter was old—no, *ancient* was a better word. And black—no, *ebony*—with keys that were worn from years of typing. It had written many words, sentences, and paragraphs. It was better, in a way, than any computer or word processor, because it had a history. On it Pop had written his newspaper column, *The Angler's Angle,* for twenty-five years. On it Booker could write wonderful books.

He took a deep breath and resumed typing.

Cow Captain Jersey's mouth formed a tight line. He called out the orders.

"Cow Princess Bovinia, secure Section A."

Cow Princess Bovinia hurried to secure her section of the cowship, the ship's sick bay. Princess Bovinia was the ship's doctor. She closed the medicine cabinets and the medical supply bins. As she locked them she said a prayer that they would not be needed.

A-MOO-GA! FIFTEEN SECONDS TO IMPACT!

"Booker!" his mother called from the kitchen. "Booker, have you finished your homework?"

Booker blinked, his hands poised above the keys. He didn't answer his mother. Worksheets of long division were piled neatly beside him. Three sharpened pencils lay on top of them. He would do them in a minute. He tried to stay with the story. The image of the space cows was so clear. He ignored the voice and typed on.

"First Cow Mate Angus, secure Section B!"

Angus, the ship's engineer, tightened the support straps around his tool containers. He checked the security lock on the electronics repair equipment. It would be important after the crash. It would be important, that is, if they survived.

"Booker!"

"Yes."

"Your homework! Have you finished it?"

"Almost!" he called out. The image of the space cows in his mind flickered once. If he could stall her just five more minutes . . . He typed faster.

Cow Captain Jersey strapped himself into the control seat. He checked the dials on the control panel. It was a mess of flashing warning lights and whirling dials.

"All ship personnel prepare yourselves for impact."

SIX

FIVE

FOUR

"Booker, I hear that typewriter. Now you turn it off and get to your homework."

Footsteps echoed across the dining room floor. He didn't have to look to see the image of his mother in the sweatpants and T-shirt she always seemed to wear lately, strands of hair drooping tiredly from her ponytail. He typed even faster. He had to get this one chapter done.

He knew what was coming. The electric cord to the typewriter snaked across the dining room floor. She was headed to the cord. He had to finish before she pulled the plug.

Captain Jersey took one last look at the control map. They were far off course. So far that they would never be found. They were headed toward a solar system. Toward the third planet of the solar system. A small insignificant planet called EARTH.

"Booker, are you done with that homework or not?" He heard her sigh as she paused beside the outlet. He imagined her hand holding the cord. He was almost finished.

THREE

TWO

ONE

IMPACT!

"I'm done, Mom," he called. The homework was forgotten as he pulled the last page of Chapter One out of the typewriter. "I'm done!"

2

Attack of the Sistoid

"Mo-om!"

Two feet joined his mother's blue terry-cloth slippers outside the table. The new feet wore hot-pink tennis shoes with purple polka-dot socks. Libba.

Booker began to stack the sheets of his manuscript together. He had lost his room, his bed, his space, but he still had this, his books. He tapped the small pile of paper to even the ends. There was nothing more satisfying than good writing. He opened a box of colored paper clips, selected a green one, and clipped the pages together.

"My autobiography is due next week!" the whiny voice said. The feet shifted and posed. He could imagine the rest of his big sister shifting and posing. He couldn't understand why his mother didn't seem to notice the lipstick and makeup that she had started wearing to school. Libba could get away with anything.

He on the other hand noticed everything. Noticing was part of being a good writer. His teachers back in elementary school were always saying, "Who notices something different today?" Hands would go up, but the answers would be wrong. "That picture of the dude in the wig," someone would try. "No," she would say, "George Washington has been here all year." It would be Booker who noticed that the desks had been turned to face a new direction, or that snowflakes had replaced the fall leaves on the bulletin board, or that the teacher had a new hairdo.

He looked at the feet. He would bet that his mother had not noticed that Libba had shaved her legs. Booker snickered loudly.

"Can it, dweeb brain," Libba said. She pounded the top of the table.

Libba writing? Libba's autobiography? What a joke. In his mind he began to compose it.

Under a rock deep in the darkest swamp of the planet Zon. Deep where the seven suns could not shine. Deep in the crevice under the rock, something stirred. A creature was born.

"No, Libba," his mother answered. "You can't have it."

"I *need* it, Mom."

He halfheartedly followed the conversation going on above him. He got a lot of good ideas from listening in on conversations. Eavesdropping was another one of the skills necessary to become a good writer.

Usually Libba's conversation was not worthy dialogue. Once, during the writing of *The Planet of the*

Teenage Robotoids, he had listened to her talk on the telephone. Hoping for a bit of dialogue crucial to his story, he'd crouched, hidden in her closet on top of the twenty-five pairs of shoes and cheerleader pompoms, with his notebook.

Finally she made a call. He had counted the number of times that she said the words "No way." He got up to thirty before his mother rescued him by calling them to dinner.

Libba was boring. But Libba's autobiography— that was interesting.

```
    It crawled forth, not man or beast, not
fish or fowl. A hideous creature. A creature so
evil it could only be called . . . Sistoid.
```

"But Mr. Geddis says I'll get extra credit if I type it."

Type!

Booker listened more closely now. The feeling of security that he usually got from his tent evaporated.

He placed his hands on either side of the ancient ebony typewriter. It was still warm from the writing that he had done for his first chapter.

They couldn't take his typewriter away. Could they?

"Mom, I have to have it."

"Now, Libba, we've already taken his room," his mother said. "The only reason he agreed to move into the dining room was because we promised him the typewriter. It's not fair to take the typewriter too."

12

Booker nodded in agreement. His mother was right. Libba was not the one who had given up her room when Pop broke his hip, Booker was. The least they could do was to keep their promise to him. He felt like a Ping-Pong match was being played on the table above him; the words were like the ball bouncing back and forth.

Ping!

"Do you want me to *fail* language arts? Maybe even fail eighth grade? You said yourself for me to do my best."

Pong!

"I don't think that would cause you to fail."

Ping!

"I mean, those autobiographies are half our language arts grade."

Silence.

His mother missed the ball.

He crawled out from under the table and blinked. He clutched his manuscript against his chest.

"It's mine, Mom! You promised."

"Now, Booker," his mother said.

Libba gave him a quick slant-eyed look. "I need it," she said. "You don't."

"I do need it." He tried to keep his voice calm. "I really need it." His voice went up a few notes higher. "Really."

"He doesn't need it. He's playing with it. I need it for something important."

"My books are important. Writing is important."

"Not your writing, dweeb brain."

"That's enough, Libba," his mother said.

"So, Mom. Do you want me to pass language arts or not?"

His mother put her hands on her hips and sighed. She gave Booker a sort of helpless look. "I wish your father were home," she said. "I just don't know."

"If we wait for Dad to decide," Libba said, "I'll fail for sure! Dad's never home anymore." She grabbed at the manuscript in Booker's hand. He pulled back but too late. She snatched the pages away.

"'A-moo-ga! A-moo-ga!'" she read aloud. "Mom, does this sound like important writing?"

"Libba, give Booker's writing back to him."

"'Warning lights flashed on the cowship.'" Smiling an evil smile, Libba held the pages up out of his reach and shook them. "'The ship blasted through darkest space.'"

"That's enough, Libba," his mother said in a tired voice. "Booker, give the typewriter to Libba, just for this week. I worry about you spending too much time under that table anyway."

"We could wait for Dad to decide," Booker tried. "That's a good idea." He knew even as he said it that it wouldn't work. His father had not been home before Booker's bedtime for over a month. The only evidence that he had been in the house at all was a coffee cup at his place every morning at the breakfast table. You don't get much support from a coffee cup.

His mother sighed. "Libba, you can have it this week, then Booker gets it back next week."

Booker jumped and made a desperate grab for the papers.

"Booker!"

"Yes."

"I said to give the typewriter to your sister. She needs it this week. Libba, you give Booker's writing back."

"Take it," Libba said. She tossed the pages into the air and they showered down around the table. "Take your precious book!" She reached under the table and pulled the typewriter out, jerking the cord from the wall with one swift movement.

"*A-moo-ga,*" she said over her shoulder as she strutted out of the dining room and down the hall toward her bedroom, the long cord waving behind her like a tail.

The battle of the Sistoid was over and he had lost.

Sistoid crept out from under the rock and changed the universe. A change for the worse. It was a creature destined to bring misery to be-ings of higher intelligence everywhere.

Booker Jones
Pickle Springs, AR
March 20

Hamerstein Books
New York, NY

Dear Editor,
Enclosed is the first chapter of my

newest book, SPACE COWS! The best book in the history of the universe!

WORMS FROM THE PLANET SPAGHETTI was a big mistake. The problem? The characters. It is hard for the reader to get into the mind of a worm. It is also difficult for the writer to get into the mind of a worm. Forget I ever sent it to you.

MOON MUMMY was boring. I admit it. The problem? The setting. How many ways can you describe the moon? Is it gray, gray, or gray? I tried it out on my sixth-grade class. Three kids shot me with rubber bands and Jon Birdsong fell asleep on Chapter Three. It's the first time in the history of Pickle Springs Middle School that a class was happy when math started. (See, I can be funny too!) Forget about MOON MUMMY. It was not my best work.

As they say, three is a charm. So with that in mind I am sending you the beginning of the best book in the history of the universe: SPACE COWS!

But enough—I don't want to spoil the story for you, so go ahead, turn the page and read it for yourself!

Udderly yours,

Booker Jones
Author-in-Training

My Father
the Coffee Cup

"Booker, have you had breakfast?"

"Your concern is touching."

Booker still would not look at his mother. He had managed to go through dinner, the rest of the evening, and now the morning without once making eye contact. He had still not forgiven her betrayal. His only consolation was that one chapter at least was finished and ready for mailing. He would send it with his letter after school.

Booker paused briefly by the kitchen table to grab a handful of Krispy Krunchies out of the box.

"That's crude," Libba commented from her spot at the table as he tossed them into his mouth. Her hair was pulled back in a ponytail tied with a green ribbon. Two pink curlers dangled optimistically from the ponytail. She pressed a white paper napkin to her lips as if she were the Queen Mother.

"Mom, Booker's eating out of the cereal box," she said.

He took one more handful in defiance. His mother looked up from the counter where she was trying to make room for Pop's breakfast tray among the piles of unopened mail and dirty dishes. She looked for a moment like she was trying to think of something. Then the microwave beeped and she turned to remove Pop's morning bowl of oatmeal.

Booker noticed an empty coffee cup at his father's place. The cup bore the name of his father's sign shop, Signs of the Times. All the cups that they used at home were rejects from the shop—like the coffee mug with a slightly off-center photo of a pet poodle and a botched Wally Way Motors cup.

It was as if his father himself had turned into a coffee cup, like a movie that Booker had seen once about a man who became a fly. He made a mental note to put it in his file of ideas for future books. He would call it *My Father the Coffee Cup*.

It began in the morning, pretty much like any other morning . . . at first. The man looked in the mirror, combing his hair. Blow-drying it carefully into place. He hummed as he combed.

Clink!

He stopped, dread filling his body. He combed once again.

Clink! The sound again. The sound seemed to be the comb hitting his ear. But . . .

Slowly he raised his hands. He parted his hair. In place of his ear was a porcelain handle.

Could it be? No it couldn't, but it was.
He was turning into a

"Have you got your lunch money?"

"Huh?" Booker's head snapped up.

"Have you got your money?"

Booker nodded.

"Your homework?"

"He never does his homework, Mom." Libba speared a piece of banana from her cereal and held it up to examine it. She sighed. "I'm sooooo tired . . ." she said dramatically, looking at Booker with eyes like slits. ". . . from *typing*." She ate the banana piece.

He tossed a few Krunchies in her direction.

"Thank you," she said.

He had passed by Libba's room that morning. The sight of the typewriter was torture. The sound of her slowly pecking one key, then another, was worse.

He had read once that a writer named James Dickey bought a new typewriter every time he started a new book. Booker had understood completely. There was nothing like writing on a typewriter.

In the same article he had read that Robert Ludlum would write only with a Ticonderoga No. 2 pencil. He made a mental note to stop by the Pencil Box Shop at school to see if they had any Ticonderoga No. 2 pencils. If he couldn't type, he could at least use the proper pencils.

His mind jumped ahead, frantically thinking of ways to keep his book going. Cynthia Rylant always wrote on yellow legal pads. Maybe he could get some of those, too.

"Typing is sooooo tiring," Libba repeated.

"Well," Booker responded, "it's only tiring for two fingers, because that's all you use."

"I do not."

"I saw you." Booker did a perfect imitation of her typing method.

"That's enough, kids," his mother said. "Libba, take this tray to your grandfather."

"It's Booker's turn," Libba complained.

"I did it yesterday."

"Did not."

His mother sighed and picked up the tray herself. "I don't have the energy to fight with you two," she said.

"Now see what you did," Libba said as they watched their mother, who was still dressed in her faded cotton bathrobe, walk out with the tray. "You made Mom mad . . . again."

Booker felt no guilt, only relief. He would do anything to stay out of his old bedroom. He had thought when Pop moved in that it would be great. Pop had an appreciation for words and stories that no one else in the family had. After all, Pop was a writer, a real writer, a published writer, like Booker would be someday.

Pop lived, breathed, and wrote fishing. "Write about what you care about," he had once told Booker. Pop cared about fishing. A river bubbled past Pop's cottage, the Write House. It flowed over rocks and boulders, twisting in long braids of gleaming water. Pop and the river had always seemed inseparable. In the summer, Pop fished. Booker could see Pop standing hip deep in the water, casting out long ribbons of fishing line over and over, like a lion tamer cracking his whip at the circus, only more graceful—a ballet with the water.

In the winter, when Pop couldn't fish, he built giant, roaring fires in the stone fireplace at the Write House and typed out stories and articles about fish on the old typewriter. While he typed, Booker and Libba worked jigsaw puzzles on an old rusty card table in front of the fire.

Booker loved Pop's columns. He saved them in a green leather notebook. His grandfather had a way of saying things that meant just the opposite. If Pop wanted to complain about the traffic at the river, he praised the sound of the traffic.

Ah, opening day of trout season on the Little Red River. The sounds of nature. The peaceful call of the Volvo station wagon, the hum of the wild Mercedes, the gentle purring of a BMW.

The Pop that Booker remembered didn't seem to have anything to do with the man lying silent and still in Booker's bed.

Booker took one more handful of Krunchies and headed for the door. "Mo-om," he heard Libba call out as the screen door slammed behind him. "Booker didn't eat breakfast."

He jogged down the front steps and across the

21

lawn to the sidewalk. He glanced back at his house and was surprised at how normal it looked. A small, one-level, brick ranch house identical to every other house on their street—from the outside.

The farther away he moved from his house the better he felt, like a prisoner swimming away from Alcatraz. Each step took him farther from Libba and his mother and Pop. The thought of his chapter packaged and ready for mailing in his book bag cheered him.

He tried to think of the right word to describe the feeling that he got as he moved away from the house. He felt light—no, *buoyant* was a better word. And free—no, *unfettered*. It was always important to use the correct word.

Up ahead at the corner he could see the bus-stop crowd. He could tell that his best friend, Germ, was excited about something, as usual. Germ, the smallest boy in the sixth grade, seemed to make up for his lack of size with motion. Booker could see his hands slicing the air in karate chops of enthusiasm. Booker stretched his arms out, enjoying the space around him, as he hurried, buoyant and unfettered, to join the action.

4

Boom!

"Hey, Bookworm!" Germ spotted Booker and waved his arms in wide arcs. "You hear about the Wolf Pack?" Germ's size combined with the last name Germondo gave him his unfortunate nickname.

"*Aaaooooooo!*" Booker yelled. The Wolf Pack was the mascot for Pickle Springs Middle School, and whenever anyone said the words *Wolf Pack* everyone howled.

Booker smoothed down his wrinkled T-shirt as he walked. On the front was printed TOO MANY BOOKS, SO LITTLE TIME. He hoped no one would notice how many times he had worn it this week. He pulled his denim jacket tighter around him. The morning air was cool and damp.

"You read the paper?" Germ yelled. He walked toward Booker with bounding strides, as if he could add inches to his height by the sheer force of his steps.

"No," said Booker. He thought of the pile of newspapers unread on his front porch.

"PTO met last night." Germ met Booker and turned to walk with him.

"So?"

"So I thought your mother was something big in the PTO."

"She was," Booker answered. "Second vice president or something like that. Now she's too busy."

"She didn't go to the meeting?"

Booker shook his head. "What happened?"

"They want to change the name of the school mascot."

"No way!"

"Wait, it gets worse."

"It can't be worse," said Booker. "They want to get rid of the Wolf Pack?"

Three kids at the bus stop howled. *"Aaoooooooo!"*

"You haven't heard what they want to change it to."

"What?"

"You won't believe it."

"What?"

"You're not going—"

"Tell me!"

"The Fighting Pickles."

There was a moment of silence as they walked the last few steps together to the group of kids at the bus stop.

"You're joking, right?" Booker said. "Fact? Or fiction?"

He had learned long ago not to trust everything

that Germ said. Germ was the only kid he knew who had a more vivid imagination than he himself did.

"Fact!" Germ said. He held his hand in front of his face like a microphone. "Yes, folks," he said in a deep voice, "today is a sad day for all the students of Pickle Springs Middle School. The Wolf Pack is doomed."

"Aaooooooo!" They all pointed their faces upward and howled a sad howl.

Germ dropped the imaginary mike.

"Why would they even want to change it?" Booker asked.

"Well, it's unfair to wolves they said at the meeting. It makes them seem too violent. But the real reason is that the Pickle family is donating a new athletic field."

"You've got to be kidding," Booker said. "Isn't it enough that they named the town after themselves?"

"And don't forget the golf course," Germ added. "We've got to stop them."

"Who's *we?*"

"You and me! You know, we're a team—like Siskel and Ebert, Calvin and Hobbes . . ."

"Beavis and Butt-head?" Booker offered.

"Ha ha. There's an open PTO meeting next week at the school for the parents and teachers to vote on the change. If the PTO wants it we're sunk. So, we'll organize all the kids to come before the meeting for a rally. Maybe we can get the radio station to come. You in?"

Booker thought a moment. They had always been the Wolf Pack. You shouldn't change history just because

25

someone named Pickle likes the sound of his name. "I'm in."

"We need some signs!" Germ said, waving his arms. "Some slogans!" He was a great organizer.

The bus pulled up and groaned to a stop. Booker and Germ got into the line that slowly moved forward to get on the bus.

"Hey, Bookworm. I've got it!" Germ said.

"What?"

"A slogan. Pickle Springs Middle School . . ." He paused for effect. ". . . is in a pickle."

"That's terrible."

They climbed into the bus and sat together on one of the worn leather seats. The bus jerked forward with a groan.

Germ rubbed the fog off the window with the arm of his jacket. "You think of something, Booker. You're the writer." He turned around in his seat and called out to the other kids. "How many of you wimps are going to help save the Wolf Pack?"

"*Aaaaooooooo!*" every kid on the bus yelled.

As they rode toward school, Germ led a cheer. His thin arms punctuated the air as he yelled.

"Gimme a W."

"W!" the kids answered.

"Gimme an O."

"O!"

"Gimme an L. . . ."

Booker liked being with Germ. When he was with Germ, he didn't have to talk much. Even when Germ asked him questions, most of the time he didn't expect Booker to answer. Germ often answered the questions himself.

"If you could have any kind of car in the world, what would you pick?" he would say. "A red Ferrari," he'd answer before Booker could even open his mouth. Germ filled up the silence around Booker and let him think.

Booker's mind shifted back and forth between pickles and space cows. Pickles and space cows. Pickles and space cows. The space cows won.

Booker imagined the beginning of Chapter Two. He would start with a big explosion. It would start out with one word—one giant word:

BOOM!

Booker pulled out his notebook and began to write.

First there was only darkness. Smoke. A small fire in the rear of the ship. And silence.

No one moved on the cowship. No one raised a hoof.

Captain Jersey opened his eyes and looked around at the damage. He unsnapped his seat belt.

"Bovinia!" he called out.

"Here, Captain!"

"Are you all right?"

"Yes."

"Angus?"

"Right here, sir."

Captain Jersey's face drew down into a grim frown. The mission was lost.

The mission? What mission?

The space cows needed a mission. Booker tried to imagine what would be important to space cows.

The quest for the perfect grass.

No, too boring.

The search for a new planet to inhabit.

No, already done too many times.

"Hey, Bookworm," Germ said. The cheer was over. "I have an idea."

"Uh huh." Booker had a special way of closing out all conversation around him. He had found that if he said "Uh huh" over and over people didn't know that he wasn't listening. He had learned this from his mother who often used this technique herself.

Germ kept talking.

"Uh huh," Booker answered, keeping the story flowing in his mind. He thought of the mission.

The mission—to determine if there was intelligent cow life on other planets. So far the answer had been no.

They had visited the planet Butteria.

NO INTELLIGENT COW LIFE.

They had visited the planet Mooia. Again the sad report:

NO INTELLIGENT COW LIFE.

Again and again the crew had landed. Five hundred and forty planets, and always the same answer:

NO INTELLIGENT COW LIFE.

"So it's okay?" Germ said.

"Uh huh," Booker answered.

"Great!" Germ said.

Booker blinked. He closed his notebook. "Is what okay?" he said.

Germ wasn't listening now. He was standing up, waving his arms. "Hey!" he said. "Booker, our famous writer, has agreed to write a speech for the rally!"

"Yay!" the other kids cheered.

Booker grabbed Germ's arm and pulled him back down into the seat. "You know I'm working on a new book."

"Yeah, that's why I was so surprised when you said you'd do it."

"I can't—"

"Hey," Germ interrupted, "you're a writer, remember? Are you saying you can't write a speech?"

"Of course I'm not." Booker slumped low in his seat. "I can easily write a speech. Piece of cake. I could do it in my sleep. But I've got to finish my book first."

"No problem," Germ said. "You have a whole week to write the speech." Then his microphone was back in place. "Broadcasting live from the Pickle Springs Middle School bus, this is Germ Germondo."

Three spit wads flew through the air and hit Germ before he could finish. He fell dramatically back against the seat, his hands clutched to his chest in a dying pose.

Booker scowled at Germ. He had trapped him. Because of Germ, the thing that writers call a "deadline" had now complicated his life. A week did not sound like a very long time.

At least he had accomplished *something* during the bus ride. He had finished Chapter Two—well, almost. He liked to end his chapters with a hook. Something to keep the reader wondering. Something to make the reader turn the page to Chapter Three. He looked down at his notebook and added a few more lines.

"Captain, what's wrong?" Angus said. "You look worried."

"Look at this dial, Angus. It seems to be a small timer." The captain pointed his hoof to a small clock on the control panel that he had not noticed before.

"Bad news, Captain. It _is_ a timer and it's ticking. We must complete our search and repair the ship in one week or . . ."

"Or what?"

"Or the ship will self-destruct. We now have a deadline."

"Can we do it, Captain?" Bovinia asked in a worried voice.

Captain Jersey sighed. "We can only try."

5

Intelligent Cow Life

Save the Wolf Pack!

A petition was quietly being circulated during math class.

The undersigned students of Pickle Springs Middle School vote to save the Wolf Pack.

There were already forty-three signatures from the morning.

After eyeing the chalkboard at the front of the room to check that Mr. Filippone's back was turned, Booker signed the petition and passed it on. Then his gaze returned to the chalkboard, which was covered with mysterious long-division problems. They had no more meaning to Booker than ancient hieroglyphics.

Mr. Filippone pointed at the problems one by one with a long stick. His brown curly hair bounced and his dark eyebrows lifted with each jab. He said, "Place value! Place value!"

Booker had noticed that Mr. Filippone seemed to have only five shirts. When he was in a good mood he wore the pink golf shirt. When he wore the white oxford cloth shirt with the worn elbows—look out. Today he had on the pink golf shirt. He was very excited about the numbers on the board.

Booker opened his spiral notebook. He glanced once at Mr. Filippone and began to write.

Chapter Three

The space cows peered out the window at the planet called Earth. There were green fields and trees. The sky was blue, filled with puffy white clouds.

Could they by accident have stumbled on the planet that they had spent twelve lunar years seeking? A planet with intelligent cow life?

"Hey, Bookworm!"

Booker looked up from his notebook.

Haines Wilson passed him a white sheet of paper.

"I already signed . . ." Booker stopped. It wasn't the petition.

He looked at the words on the top of the page and his heart sank. CHAPTER TEST. The long division problems stretched out forever on the paper.

"Hey." He tapped Haines on the back. "How do you—"

"No talking!" called Mr. Filippone.

Booker looked at the first problem: $65\overline{)432}$. He blinked and looked around. Everyone else was filling out answers.

He glanced at his notebook, then back at the test. There was no way he could do the problems on the page. Still, he tried the first one. 65 goes into 432 how many times? He wrote down 0. Then he erased it.

It was hopeless. He looked at the notebook and back at his test. He might as well ... No—he really shouldn't ... He turned back to the notebook. He would write for just a few minutes. Writing always cleared his mind. It would be like a warm-up exercise. Then he would start the problems. He began to write.

Captain Jersey tried to conceal the excitement in his voice. "Call up the conditions for cow life on the computer."

The voice of the computer began to list the conditions for cow life.

Fact One: Climate must contain a gas level comprised of 80% nitrogen, 20% oxygen.

Captain Jersey nodded. "Angus, check the gas level."

"Yes, sir."

Angus pushed a silver button on the cabin wall. After a few seconds he released the button and a tape clicked out of the control panel. He ripped it off and read:

"80% nitrogen, 20% oxygen."

They exchanged excited looks. The gas level was correct.

"Ten more minutes," Mr. Filippone announced.

Booker's pencil hesitated above his notebook. He glanced at the test. Then the pencil was drawn back to the story as if pulled by some powerful magnetic force.

Fact Two: The planet must have a temperate climate—between 25 and 98 degrees Fahrenheit.

"Have we tested the temperature?" Captain Jersey asked.

"Yes, sir," Bovinia answered as she looked down at a dial. "75 degrees."

Again they paused and looked at each other. The temperature was correct.

Fact Three: H_2O must be available.

"Is water available?"

They looked at the puffy white clouds in the sky of the planet.

"Yes, Captain."

Fact Four: There must be a source of vegetation.

They stared out at the field of grass in front of them.

They were silent for a moment.

Captain Jersey cleared his throat. "My conclusion," he said, "is that cow life is possible on this planet."

"Your test, please?"

The bell had rung. Everyone had gone to lunch and Booker was alone in the classroom with Mr. Filippone. He slammed his notebook closed.

"My test?"

"Yes, your chapter test. Some of my students have been working on it for the last thirty minutes." He tugged his mustache.

"Oh, yeah . . . That's my favorite of your shirts, Mr. Filippone."

"What's wrong with the others?" Mr. Filippone's mouth turned up just a bit at the corners in what might have been a smile.

"Nothing, they're all great."

"Enough talking about my shirts, Booker. But thank you for the compliment." The corners dropped. "We should be talking about your test." He held out his hand. "I'd like to have it now."

Booker swallowed. He handed Mr. Filippone the empty paper. He had erased so hard on the first problem that there was a big hole above the division problem.

"Booker, I've been wanting to talk to you." Mr. Filippone sat down on top of the empty desk beside Booker.

"You have?"

"About your math. I haven't been getting any homework back from you."

"Long division came along at what you might call a bad time," Booker said.

"Oh? Is there a problem at home? Something I should know about?"

"No, it's just my brain's kind of—I don't know how to explain it. I feel like my brain has made all the adjustments it can handle."

"Well, math isn't your best subject, I admit that, but you always manage."

"I know. I can't explain it." He almost added, *You'd have to be living under a dining room table to understand it.*

He didn't even understand it himself. Only four weeks ago everything in his life had been perfect. His room carefully organized, with everything in place. His desk with ten sharpened pencils and three tablets centered on top. His library of books organized by author's last name on his shelves. He'd thought of it as a studio. A writer's retreat. And suddenly it was all gone.

Everything had changed. It had been dramatic and fast, like the opening of a book.

The setting had been breakfast. It had started just like any of thousands of breakfasts at his house—his father pouring coffee, his mother calling out headlines of interest from the *Pickle Springs Press*. MARJORIE WATTS PLANNING A TRIP TO HOT SPRINGS. DOUGLAS MORNINGTON GROWS SQUASH SHAPED LIKE MOUNT RUSHMORE.

The phone rang. His mother answered. There was a long pause, then she said, "No." Then a pause. Then another "No." Then another pause and a "No."

He had sat with his father and sister at the kitchen table trying to fill in the blanks. It was amazing how so much meaning could come through one small word. The *no*'s were *no*'s of disbelief and protest, like someone might say in one of his books:

A giant superkinetic blob was moving toward the city.
"No!"

Or:

The town of Pickle Springs had been surrounded by extraterrestrial aliens.
"No!"

She had then turned and summed up the conversation in two inadequate words. "Pop fell."

His parents had sent him to school while they traveled to the hospital to meet the ambulance. One week later they had brought Pop home. The boxes had come soon after. His nightstand was now covered with medicine bottles and dirty glasses. Pop had moved in and suddenly Booker had found himself living in the dining room. It was hard to do long division under a dining room table.

"You know you can come to me if you don't understand something."

"I know."

There was a pause.

"Well, you let me know if there's anything I can do. I'm always here."

Booker nodded. He had stopped caring about his work at school, like his mother had stopped caring for the plants in the dining room. It just didn't seem to matter much anymore.

In *The Battle of the Teenage Robotoids* Booker had invented something called the stealth cloud. The stealth cloud would come over perfectly normal people and take away their desire to do anything but eat pizza and listen to rock music. Now Booker felt like he was under his own personal stealth cloud. It had come over him and had taken away his desire to do anything but lose himself in his writing.

He didn't think Mr. Filippone would understand and he couldn't imagine his parents understanding either. He had a sudden fearful thought that Mr. Filippone might write a note to his mother about his problems in math.

"What do you think about the Fighting Pickles?" Booker said abruptly, hoping to divert Mr. Filippone's attention.

Mr. Filippone crossed his arms. The test was crumpled in one hand now and tucked, forgotten, under his arm. "Things change," he said.

"But we've always been the Wolf Pack. It's not fair to change it just because somebody named Pickle thinks it would be a blast to hear a lot of people yelling 'Yay Pickles.' The Wolf Pack is a part of history, like the Washington Monument or the American flag."

"The American flag has changed many times, Booker," Mr. Filippone said with a smile. "Nothing's forever."

"I know," said Booker. "But... it doesn't seem fair." He was surprised at how much he suddenly cared. He was reliving the same feeling of frustration he felt when his parents took his room away. He caught his breath and continued. "It doesn't seem right that parents can decide whatever they want. They don't even ask us what we think and we have to go along with it."

"Welcome to reality."

Booker thought for a moment, then said quietly, "If that's reality, I like fiction better."

Mr. Filippone stood up and brushed the chalk dust from his pants. "You want my unofficial advice?"

"Yeah."

"If you care about it, do something about it."

Booker walked out of the room wondering what he *could* do about it. Before he could think of anything to do, the next paragraph of his book popped into his mind instead and he stopped in the hall to pull out his notebook and write.

The space cows began to arm themselves for battle. They watched the white clouds blow by across the sky. They did not know what to expect in this new, ever-changing planet. Whatever it was, they would be ready.

6

Arrest That Coffee Cup!

"Let me guess." The man behind the counter at the post office looked down at Booker and held out his hand to accept the brown envelope. "New York, right?"

Booker lifted the package gently, like you would lift a baby. He suddenly remembered an old photograph in his baby book of his father standing by his mother and lifting him like that. His parents had gazed down at him, a tiny bundle in a droopy white blanket, with beaming smiles. Their faces had seemed to glow. Their expressions were—he searched for the correct word—*resplendent*. He was sure his own face was resplendent as he looked at the envelope on the post office scale.

"Two ninety," the man said.

Booker dug into his pocket and dumped a collection of quarters and dimes onto the counter. "You sure it'll get there okay?"

The man nodded.

"You won't lose it?"

Suddenly it seemed like the most valuable package in the world. The man at the counter, oblivious to its true importance, stamped the envelope and tossed it unceremoniously onto the pile of brown packages at his feet.

"Careful," Booker said. Obviously to the man it appeared to be a plain ordinary envelope, but to Booker the envelope was hope. Hope that this time, after twenty-two tries, he would finally be recognized as a writer.

In the past the hope had not been fulfilled. He had mailed the other twenty-two books off in their brown envelopes one by one. He had waited. And waited. And waited. The end result was always the same. A brown envelope would come to the door with his book in it.

Usually it had a letter attached to it that said *Sorry, your book does not meet the needs of our list.* Booker didn't know exactly what that meant except that it meant no, they didn't want to publish his book.

This one, the start of the best book in the history of the universe, would be a different story.

Booker left the post office and blinked in the afternoon sun. He began to walk toward home, then turned and headed toward the sign shop. He had felt an empty spot all morning thinking about his father and how long it had been since he had seen him. He could see the sign shop at the end of the street with his father's brown Chevy parked outside.

He stopped by the car and cupped his hands on the windshield to look inside. The floor of the car was littered with white fast-food bags and napkins and trash.

Resting on the seat in front of the steering wheel was a white ceramic coffee mug. It was as if the cup had been driving!

The brown Chevy roared past the police car as if it were standing still. The man driving the Chevy stepped on the gas. He had to save himself. He had to get to the hospital. His wife's words echoed in his brain:

"Dear, you seem a little . . ." She had paused. ". . . cylindrical today."

Now the handle in his ear had grown and everything else seemed to be shrinking.

Officer Mark turned on his blue light and raced after the speeding car. His siren roared. "Pull over," he called on the bullhorn. "We've got you surrounded."

He hurried up to the window of the Chevy with his deputy. "You're under arrest for reckless driving," he said as he looked into the window.

"Uh . . ." He took a second look. The man was gone!

"Book him . . . uh . . . Book it," he said to his deputy as he stared at the coffee cup on the seat.

"Arrest that coffee cup!"

Booker shook his head. He turned and paused for a moment outside the plate-glass window of the store. Mrs. Mooney, who worked at the store with his father, was feeding stacks of paper into a large copy machine and cradling the telephone under her neck as she worked. Her gray hair bounced as she nodded yes into the phone. No sign of his father.

A bell tinkled as he pushed open the glass door. Mrs. Mooney waved a piece of paper at him in welcome. "I'll have that order to you by tomorrow for sure," she was saying into the phone. "No more delays this time, I promise.

"Hi, Booker," she said as she hung up. "Your father—" She stopped as the phone rang again, then picked up the receiver. "Signs of the Times . . . Yes . . ."

Booker looked around the shop at the shelves with neatly organized piles of colored paper and large bottles of paint and ink. The floor was spotless, and the machines hummed in an orderly way—not like his house. He understood now why his father wasn't coming home and didn't blame his dad, really. He, too, escaped as often as possible. Every weekend since Pop moved in he had spent Friday or Saturday night with Germ. Until Pop moved in, he had not appreciated the luxury of sleeping in a real bed. Germ's bunk beds, as creaky and lumpy as they were, were heaven compared to the floor.

He thought of the fast-food bags in his father's car. Mrs. Germondo cooked, really cooked, like his mother used to—with flour and salt and other real ingredients. Not like his mother did now, heating up things in foil pans she'd bought from the frozen-food section. She didn't bake, she thawed.

After one particularly long stay at Germ's—two nights without coming home—his mother had stopped allowing him to spend the night with Germ. "You're imposing," she'd said. "We can't pay them back. We don't have room to invite Germ here."

Now his only escape was his books.

"Booker," Mrs. Mooney said as she hung up the phone, "your dad's stepped out to deliver some campaign posters for the mayor."

"Can I wait?" he asked.

"Sure. Have a seat." She pointed to his dad's white desk, where a brown coffee mug sat in the middle of the green blotter.

Booker sat down, rolled the chair around into position, and touched the coffee mug gently. He picked up one of the pens and began to doodle on the pad of paper in front of him. He could work a little on his speech. He drew a pickle. *The fighting pickles,* he wrote. He stopped and marked the words out. He needed a more impressive beginning.

He remembered an exercise that he had learned in a writing class at school. Around the pickle he began to write things about pickles. *Green, bumpy, tasty.*

He tried again.

The green, bumpy, tasty pickles . . .

He marked that out too. The pickle in his picture seemed to stare at him, and he crumpled the paper. No need to work on the speech now. He had an entire week to do it.

"Mrs. Mooney," he called, "do you know when my dad will be back?"

She shook her head.

"Can I use the computer?" He loved to type on his father's computer.

"Sure," she said. "You know how to turn it on?"

Booker nodded. He flipped a switch and a few keystrokes later he was with the space cows again.

Chapter Four

"Look!" Bovinia called excitedly. "Look, Captain!"

"Yes?"

Captain Jersey looked down at the ground. A smile spread across his face. "At last," he said. "After twelve lunar years of travel, after wars and pig aliens, this..." He gestured to the ground below them.

The print of a cow hoof was pressed into the warm dirt.

"Come, we must find this Earth cow."

Bovinia and Captain Jersey hurried farther down the path.

This was almost as good as his typewriter. Booker looked away from the computer screen and saw that Mrs. Mooney had moved over to the T-shirt counter, where she was pressing numbers onto a pile of maroon Little League jerseys.

"You need some help?" Booker called out.

She shook her head. "This is it for today."

"You think Dad will be back soon?"

"Any minute."

Booker turned back to the screen.

"Captain!" Bovinia gazed through the bushes. "Look!"

"Can it be?"

"It can."

"Is it possible?"

"It is."

Together they said the three most important words:

"Intelligent Cow Life!"

The phone rang.

"Booker?" Mrs. Mooney held the phone away from her ear and called to him.

"Yes?"

"It's your dad. He's got to go to the warehouse and he won't be back at the shop today."

"Oh."

"He said he'll see you at home."

"Right." Booker sighed. He punched the *print* button, watched as a white piece of paper rolled out of the printer, and turned off the computer. He took the paper and put it into his book bag, and then he moved the brown coffee cup back into its position in the middle of the desk.

"Bye, Dad," he said softly to the cup.

"You say something?" Mrs. Mooney asked.

Booker stood up, shaking his head, and hurried out the door.

Booker Jones
Pickle Springs, AR

March 23

Hamerstein Books
New York, NY

Dear Editor,

As you make your decision about my newest and most excellent book, SPACE COWS, I thought you might like to have a little background information on me, the author.

You can tell from my name, BOOKer, that I will be the perfect author. My real name is Walter but because of my love of books everyone calls me Booker. I loved books at a young age. As a baby I teethed on GOOD NIGHT MOON. My friends even call me Bookworm. You can put that on the jacket flap along with my biography.

I was born in the town of Pickle Springs. I reside (temporarily) under the dining room table. Likes: writing, books, home cooking, my own bed. Dislikes: Long division, writing speeches, sisters.

About illustrators. I would like to request Maurice Sendak or Gary Larson. If Maurice and Gary are not available maybe my best friend Germ Germondo could do it. He got an A in art.

Hope to hear good news from you soon.

Factually yours,

Booker Jones
Bibliophile

7

Space Cows in Washington

As the days of the week passed, Booker imagined his manuscript traveling toward New York City. The first day it would have stayed in the Pickle Springs Post Office. The second it would have traveled to the larger post office in Little Rock. Then on an airplane to New York. Then from the airport to the publishing company. By now, Saturday morning, it was there.

Booker sat under the dining room table reading.

"Mo-om," he heard Libba say in the kitchen.

"Just a minute, Libba."

"All the cheerleaders are going to the mall but me."

"Now, Libba—"

"We're supposed to buy brown cloth for the Wolf Pack rally. We're making three hundred rally rags."

All was as normal at the University Mall. A darkness descended. Sistoid oozed into Penney's, and the mall was never the same.

"Libba, I can't leave your grandfather."

"Where's Dad?"

"Your dad's at work."

"On Saturday?"

"On Saturday."

Booker wondered for a moment if the editors in New York worked on Saturday. He closed his eyes and imagined the editor opening his envelope. The small picture of the space cow that he had drawn beside the return address would have caught his attention first. Then he would open the envelope and begin to read.

"Hey!" he would call out the open door of his office. "Come here, everyone! We have a winner!"

The other editors would gather around and he would read it out loud.

"Awesome!"

"Fantastic!"

"We'll take it!"

"Call that writer Booker Jones and tell him to send the rest of the book. And sign him up for the *Today* show!"

"Booker!"

Two blue slippers appeared outside the table.

"Yes."

"Booker, I have to run Libba to the mall. Watch Pop for me."

Libba's tennis shoes arrived beside his mother's slippers. "Come on, Mom," Libba said. "Alyse is meeting me in ten minutes."

Booker looked out of the tent. "I need to finish my book," he said.

"Book-er." His mother tapped her foot. "I'm asking you to watch your grandfather this morning. You'll have all afternoon to finish your book."

Booker looked longingly at the pile of yellow legal pads and Ticonderoga No. 2 pencils beside his sleeping bag.

The book was almost finished. It was now the best eight chapters in the history of the universe. The space cows had gone through so much already. In one chapter they had been attacked by a farmer who thought they were Earth cows. He had switched them with sticks to get them into the pen. The Earth men of course did not realize that these were space cows. Captain Jersey had taken control.

"One, two, three," he had commanded. *"Levitate!"*

In another chapter Bovinia had been accidentally hooked up to a milking machine.

"Invigorating!"

His next-to-the-last chapter, "Space Cows in Washington," was coming along great. He couldn't wait to write the last chapter this afternoon. Any minute the exciting conclusion would jump into his mind and off he would go.

"Booker!"

"Yeah."

"You can't watch him under there."

"And stay out of *my* room," said Libba. "Or else."

Libba did not allow him in her room. She always had a trap for him so that she would know if he had come in or not, and the traps always worked. One time she had wet a hair and put it across her door. When he had opened the door later just to see if there were any traps, the hair fell down, unnoticed by him, to the floor. She had seen that on a spy movie. Another time she had lightly dusted the floor of her room with baby powder. Booker's footprints tiptoeing in and out of the room had been clearly visible later when Libba came home. She had taken pains each time to show him the evidence.

Booker crawled out, blinking in the light of the dining room. "I wouldn't think of going into your room. I might catch a disease."

"In case you hadn't noticed," Libba said, "my room is the cleanest room in the house."

"Yeah, but there might be ugly germs in there, because look at you."

"Mo-om, make him stop."

"Come on, Libba."

Booker watched Libba and his mother hurry toward the back door.

His mother turned back, her hand on the doorknob.

"Try reading to him, Booker."

"He won't listen."

"He will listen."

The back door slammed, and then Booker heard the car engine start. He took a pile of yellow pages and slowly walked down the hall to his old bedroom. He hesitated at the door. It didn't smell like his room anymore; it smelled a little like the clinic at school.

Pop was lying on top of the covers in his pajamas, his hands folded on his chest. He was staring at the ceiling. Booker stepped in and sat on the chair that his mother had placed at the foot of the bed.

"Pop?"

Pop didn't answer.

"Do you want to hear my book?"

No answer.

"It's a science-fiction book that I'm working on. Do you know what it's called?"

Still no answer.

"It's called *Space Cows*."

Booker began to feel like Germ. He was carrying on a conversation with himself. Pop used to love his stories. In fact he was one of the few people who did.

"Here goes," he said in a falsely cheerful voice. "*A-moo-ga! A-moo-ga!*"

He stopped reading. It didn't seem right. He leaned forward, his hands holding tighter to his story.

Booker looked more closely at his grandfather. There were things that he noticed today that he had not noticed before. The way his grandfather's skin had become pale—no, it was *transparent*. He was a vision of white. His hair was white. His skin. His faded pajamas. If this were a scene in one of his books, Booker would rewrite it, add color with his words. He would erase the words *pale* and *wan*. He would add the words *pink* and

53

robust. Erase *downcast* and write *uplifted.* Erase *tired* and write *energetic.* Erase *miserable* and write *happy.*

Pop stared off into the air like he was looking at something else beyond Booker's gray ceiling. The hand that had once tied flies and flicked a fishing rod with perfect skill now twitched in his lap.

He's somewhere else, Booker thought. *He's on the river.* He sat frozen to the seat. The pages of his book slipped one by one off of his lap.

Booker understood. Hadn't he just been on another planet? He was often transported by books and writing to another place. But he had always come back. In his mind Booker replayed Mr. Filippone's words: "Welcome to reality." As he, Booker, was being forced to emerge into a world of reality and facts, Pop was retreating to a world of fiction.

Maybe, Booker thought, living in a world of fiction was easier than living in a world of facts. He looked at the pages on the floor, his enthusiasm for his novel leaving him like the air in Mrs. Germondo's bread dough as she punched it down. He closed his eyes and sat in the silence that filled what was once his room.

How long he sat motionless on the chair he did not know. An eon? An eternity? His grandfather did not move in all that time. Pop's eyes closed finally, and his breathing turned into a snore.

Booker had an uncontrollable urge to be at his typewriter. To lose himself in his own fiction. He rose and tiptoed out of the bedroom and across the hall, hands out in typing position. He stood for a moment in the doorway of Libba's room looking at the typewriter.

He checked the door and the floor for booby traps. Then slowly, one step at a time, ignoring the danger of ugly germs, he crossed the forbidden threshold and entered Libba's room.

8

The Boy in the Black Hole

Booker tiptoed over to Libba's desk, then pressed his hands one on either side of the typewriter and eased into the chair.

There were pieces of paper crumpled on the floor around the desk and one piece of paper in the typewriter. He looked at it carefully from all angles. It could be a trap. To use the typewriter he would have to take the piece of paper out and if he did he would have to get the paper back in exactly the same spot.

He read the first line typed on the page.

I was born.

"I was born"? *This* was the important autobiography that Libba had taken away his typewriter for? He resisted the urge to add *under a rock*.

Instead he rolled the paper out and carefully counted the clicks as he rolled. Fifteen. He put it beside the desk. Then he breathed a sigh of relief. So far, so good. He rolled a fresh sheet of paper into place and flipped the *on* button.

The typewriter hummed. Music to his ears. He stretched his fingers in and out a few times. He popped his knuckles. This was what he had needed.

He closed his eyes.

"Come on, space cows," he said.

Nothing. The image of Pop lying in his bed returned.

Chapter Nine he typed. He tried to get his mind back on his writing. He stared at the page.

Nothing.

The he added.

Still nothing.

He added an *n* making it *then*.

Still his mind would not start the story. His fingers itched to type but he had nothing to say.

The phone that sat beside the typewriter suddenly rang.

Booker jumped.

It rang again.

Booby trap or no booby trap, he picked up the receiver. "Hello?" he said cautiously.

"Booker!"

"Yeah, Germ."

"You listening to the radio?"

"No."

"WPKL is having a call-in for the Wolf Pack! Turn on the radio! Right now!"

Booker reached over to Libba's clock-radio and turned it on.

"Caller Number Two, you're on."

"Cool!"

"What's your name, Caller Number Two?"

"Catherine."

"Hi Catherine, you're on the air."

"Cool!"

"Give us your thoughts on the Wolf Pack."

"Cool," she said.

"That's pathetic," Germ said into the phone. "I'm calling in. Keep listening." The phone clicked in Booker's ear.

He hung up and adjusted the dial on the radio a little louder and listened.

"Caller Number Three, you're on."

"Hi, this is Germ Germondo."

"Good to have you with us, Germ."

"I wanted to let everyone know to come to the rally right before the PTO meeting Tuesday night."

"Tell us what's going to happen."

"We're going to tell them how we feel about the Wolf Pack. We're not going to let them get away with this. We're going to tell those parents and Mr. Oxford a thing or two."

"Who's going to tell them, Germ?"

"My friend Booker Jones."

Booker turned off the radio and put his head in his hands. If he couldn't write his book, perhaps he couldn't write at all. What if he couldn't write the speech?

It was as if something had moved inside him and had taken up the place of the writing. Like the ideas and stories that had poured out of him all week were being held inside, unable to make it to the paper. It reminded him of the black holes he wrote about so often in his books. Every one of his books so far had contained one chapter called "The Black Hole." The space cows had skirted the black hole in Chapter Eight. Moon Mummy had experienced his final moment drifting into a black hole:

> Gravity swirled around Moon Mummy tighter and tighter until all light was blocked out. The mummy rotated round and round slowly in space, darkest space, deepest darkest space, sinking deeper and deeper into the black hole.

A black hole, most people believed, was empty. But he had learned in science that this was not true. A black hole was a star that had collapsed—no, the word was *imploded*. The gravitational pull of the star was so strong that none of the star's light could be seen.

That's how he felt. He had imploded. Some day, when he was able to write again, he would write about it: *The Boy in the Black Hole*.

His words to Germ now haunted him. "I can easily write a speech. Piece of cake. I could do it in my sleep."

He put in a fresh sheet of paper.

He tried to think about his speech. He closed his eyes and envisioned the crowd at the rally. When he opened his eyes, the whiteness of the blank paper was startling. He pulled it quickly out of the typewriter.

As he rose to leave he looked down at the second line of the autobiography.

It was like wonderful.

It was *like* wonderful.

Booker always hated it when people said that. It was either wonderful or it was not wonderful but it could not be *like* wonderful.

Before he could stop himself he had picked up a red pen from the desk and had drawn a line through the word *like.*

He froze. What had he done? He could not put the page back now. He had actually written on Libba's autobiography.

He heard a car door slam outside. How long had he been in here? They were already home! He had to re-type the biography before Libba came into the room. Quickly he rolled a fresh sheet of paper into place.

He counted the clicks.

Thirteen.

Fourteen.

Fifteen.

Then he typed *I was born.* It was painful to type something so boring. *It was like wonderful.*

Footsteps echoed down the hall.

Booker punched the typewriter's *off* button and quickly gathered all pages of evidence. Then he did the only thing that he could think of. He jumped into the closet, hunkered down among the twenty-two pairs of shoes and the cheerleading pompoms, and held his breath.

9

Sistoid Strikes Again

Booker crouched, barely breathing. He didn't move at all. He heard Libba come into the room and sit at the desk. Then he didn't hear anything for a while.

He shifted once, and the cheerleading pompom rustled. He cringed. Still no sound from the room. What was Libba doing?

He pressed his ear to the closet door and listened. Through the door he heard faint sounds like crying. Sistoid crying? Impossible.

Still it sounded a lot like crying to him. Small gasps first. Then loud gasps and moans.

It *was* Libba. And she was crying.

Booker was so surprised that he momentarily lost all sense of danger. Slowly he opened the door and eased out of the closet.

Libba looked up over a wad of crumpled Kleenex, her eyes red and puffy. She didn't say *"Get out!"*

Slowly he moved closer. "Libba?"

She sniffed and blew her nose.

"What's wrong?"

"This," she said. She waved a white sheet of paper in the air and let it drop onto her desk. "Mom doesn't have time to look at it. Mom doesn't have time to do anything anymore."

Booker nodded. His mother had not done much of anything lately except take care of Pop.

"Look what I found," said Libba, holding out a torn half of a piece of paper. Booker took it and read it.

Wednesday:
Cupcakes to Miss Doster's class
pick up cleaning
PTO meeting
Booker to Scouts

"It's a list that Mom wrote," Libba said. "She used to do all these things. Remember when she quit her job at the bank so she could take care of us? Now she can only take care of Pop."

"I know," Booker said, clutching at the front of his wrinkled T-shirt and holding it out. "She used to wash our clothes."

"And cook," Libba said.

"And help us with our homework. What's that?" Booker pointed to the white piece of paper on top of Libba's desk.

She handed it to him. It was the autobiography.

"It's due tomorrow," she explained. "And ... and ... and ..." Her face crumpled again. "It's ... it's ... terrible! I can't write!"

She buried her face in the tissue and sobbed. Booker stood frozen in the middle of the room experiencing an unexpected feeling of empathy with his big sister. She looked up at Booker with teary eyes, biting her bottom lip.

He actually *wanted* to help her. What could he say? The autobiography *was* terrible. For once he agreed with her. But he couldn't say that.

"Look!" She pointed at the crumpled balls of paper that covered the floor.

Booker sat down carefully on the pink spread covering Libba's bed. It was the first time he had ever sat there. The bed was crowded with stuffed animals. He squeezed in between a giant blue hippopotamus wearing a top hat and a pink flamingo.

"It can't be that bad. Let's see." Booker looked down at the paper and read the first line out loud. "I was born."

This brought on a new stream of tears.

Booker didn't know what to say. "That's not too bad." He paused, trying to think of something encouraging to add. Anything. "At least it's factual."

"You really like it?" Libba said in a small voice.

"Well, it's a beginning," Booker said, stalling for time. "And a lot of people overwrite—you know, put too much in. And as a sentence it has a lot of simplicity."

"It does?"

"Yes." He had it now. "And not only that, it has a subject and a verb."

Whew! This was tough.

He read the second line.

"It was like wonderful."

"Well," he said. "Now you've . . . uh . . . started the story."

"But," Libba cried, "it's so . . . so . . ."

Booker tried to supply the right word. "Boring?"

"No, that is not the word I was trying to think of," she answered.

"No, no, not boring. I didn't mean boring." Booker put his hand to his head. "How could I have said boring? What was I thinking of? Let's see . . ." His mind reeled. "It's not boring. It's just a little . . . anticlimactic." He caught his breath and let it out in a whoosh. That had been a close one.

Libba blinked and looked at him hard. Her eyes sharpened. It reminded him of a chameleon he had once had, right before it attacked a fly. For once his ability to find the right word had let him down. Obviously *anticlimactic,* a word choice he was proud of, had been the wrong thing to say.

"What do you mean, anticlimactic?"

"Because . . ." He grasped the flamingo's tiny pink wing for support. "You have gripped the reader with a simple, powerful sentence, *I was born,* and right away the reader wants to know more details."

"Such as?" Laser beams from her eyes pierced him.

"Where were you born?"

"Why would I need to say that?"

"What color was your baby blanket?"

"Who would care about that?"

"How did you feel when you grew up?

"Why would I put that in?"

"I just thought—"

"How dare you come in here and criticize my work!"

"You asked—"

"What makes you think you know so much about writing?"

"I just—"

"And what were you doing in my closet anyway?" Libba got up and put her hands on her hips. "Mo-om! Booker's in my room!"

He quickly jumped up and smoothed out the bedspread. Nervously he began to rearrange the animals.

"Mo-om! He was hiding in my closet!"

"But—"

"Out!"

He backed away. As he reached the doorway he was hit by a stuffed panda in a Myrtle Beach T-shirt.

"I just wanted to help."

"Out!"

The hippo flew by his head.

"You said—"

"Out!"

He got out. Some people just couldn't take creative criticism.

Booker Jones
Pickle Springs, AR
March 29

Editor
Hamerstein Books
New York, NY

Dear Editor,

This is a painful letter to write. I must inform you of a delay in the writing of the ending of my book, SPACE COWS. It is not yet the best book in the history of the universe. Right now it is only the best eight chapters in the history of the universe. Ha ha.

I am experiencing what we writers call writer's block. When I get well, I will happily send the rest of my novel.

In the words of Longfellow: "Great is the art of beginning, but greater the art is of ending." I guess even Longfellow had a little trouble with endings.

Frustratedly yours,

Booker Jones
The Boy in the
Black Hole

10

Twenty-six Letters

"What is a pickle's favorite song?"

Germ sat down next to Booker. Their class was in the media center and was supposed to be researching the Battle of Gettysburg, but everyone had pickles on their minds.

"Huh?" Booker looked up from the blank sheet of paper in front of him.

"I've decided to help you with the speech. It's always good to start with a joke. So . . . What's a pickle's favorite song?"

Booker shrugged.

" 'The Farmer in the Dill.' Get it? *Dill* pickle? The farmer in the *dill?*"

"Germ," Booker said, "that's really bad."

Germ crossed out some lines in his notebook. "You're right," he said. "That one stinks."

"Germ," Booker began.

"Yeah."

"You know how sometimes . . . I mean, like how you're having trouble writing jokes?"

"Me?" said Germ in a voice of disbelief. "Having trouble? Listen to this one if you think I'm having trouble. What's a pickle's favorite state?"

Booker didn't answer.

"Deli-ware."

"What if—say a guy had trouble writing a speech," Booker went on.

"You're saying you can't write the speech?"

"No, I didn't say that . . . exactly."

"Whew, I thought for a minute that you weren't going to write the speech. The rally's tomorrow, you know."

"Well, what if—"

"Why did the pickle cross the road?"

"I don't know." For the first time in their friendship Booker *wanted* Germ to stop talking and listen to him. The flow of words that in the past had brought comfort to Booker was now irritating.

"I don't know either," said Germ. "I haven't thought of the punch line yet." He turned back to his notebook.

Booker stared at the blank page in front of him. Still no ideas for the speech.

He now realized for the first time the true meaning of the term *writer's block*. He was pleased in a way to be suffering from an authorly kind of problem—if only he didn't have the speech to worry about. All writers, he reminded himself, at one time or another experience writer's block. He had read one time about what other writers did to overcome the problem.

Judy Blume got all her best ideas in the shower. He had already tried the shower this morning—unsuccessfully. He'd stayed under the stream of water until his fingers wrinkled and Libba turned blue yelling outside the bathroom door, but no ideas had come.

Betsy Byars would go to the library and pull down book after book and read the first line of every chapter until inspiration struck. The media center's library was his last hope. If he could only get the first line of his speech, he *knew* that the rest would come.

He glanced around. Usually his eyes went directly to the Js and the place where his own books would eventually be. Today the books were overwhelming. There were thousands of them. Thousands of writers had done it. They had come up with a first line, then a second, then a third. They had combined the twenty-six letters of the alphabet into billions of different wonderful combinations.

It would seem that with only twenty-six letters to choose from he would be able to get his own combination of letters together. But it wasn't that easy.

He stood and walked down the rows of shelves, looking for inspiration. He pulled out a book at random.

It was a dark and stormy night.

No.

He tried another.

In a hole in the ground there lived a hobbit.

No.

"Where's Papa going with that ax?"

No.

"Tom!"

No.

These were the wrong kinds of books for a speech. They only made him want to read the books.

He slipped each book back respectfully into its place. As he turned to leave, a thick, dark book caught his eye. *Famous Speeches by Famous People* was embossed in gold on the spine.

Perfect! That would surely inspire him. He pulled the book out from the shelf, impressed by the weight of it. He carried it back to his table and put it down, then glanced at the clock. Fourth period was almost over. He had about five minutes. Quickly he flipped through the pages reading the highlights of the speeches.

Fourscore and seven years ago our fathers brought forth on this continent a new nation, conceived in liberty and dedicated to the proposition that all men are created equal.

This was more like it!

Is life so dear, or peace so sweet, as to be purchased at the price of chains and slavery?

Good stuff! Great moments in history required great men and women to use words to send out a message; they required writers who cared about something and used their words to make a difference. Would he join their ranks?

He stopped at a speech from a play by William Shakespeare.

Friends, Romans, countrymen, lend me your ears;
I come to bury Caesar, not to praise him.

As Booker read the speech he began to smile. The speech was *praising* Caesar even though the speaker said it was not. It was written like Pop would write a speech. It said one thing and meant something entirely different. Booker had a new respect for William Shakespeare . . . and for Pop.

Germ glanced at the spine of the book. "Your speech will be in there one day," he said. "Maybe."

Booker closed the book. What speech? He still had no idea for his own speech. Reading the powerful words of others left him even more drained.

He remembered the words of a famous writer, Gertrude Stein: "To write is to write is to write is to write is to write is to write is to write is to write." If he could no longer write, then he was no longer a writer. No longer could he use his favorite signature: Booker Jones; writer. He had become merely Booker Jones; person.

"Why do pickles like the beach?" Germ said.

Booker shrugged.

"Because of all the sandwiches there. Get it? Sand-which-is-there? Get it?"

"I get it," said Booker.

Some people, he thought, put those twenty-six letters together better than others.

"Okay, class," Mr. Filippone called from the doorway. "Out!" He gestured toward the hall. "Time for your favorite subject."

A few kids groaned. Math.

"You will be pleased to know your chapter tests have been graded."

More groans.

"Booker."

"Yes?"

"Mr. Oxford wants to see you." Mr. Filippone held out a pink slip of paper from the office. He waved it back and forth.

Booker blinked twice. Once for the word *Mr.* and once for the word *Oxford*.

It helped his writing to visualize real people that he knew as the characters in his books. The Moon Mummy was Mr. Oxford, the principal.

That was easy to imagine. Mr. Oxford had kind of a gray look. One time Booker had been in the hall and had seen Germ sitting in math class. Booker had been standing there making faces at Germ when he had seen Germ make a face of his own, an expression of horror.

Before Booker could turn around to see what was behind him, a hand had grabbed his arm. Mr. Oxford. It had scared him so badly that his feet had actually left the floor. That afternoon he had started *Moon Mummy*.

The first paragraph of *Moon Mummy* flashed, unwelcome, into his mind.

"It's so quiet," one astronaut said to the other after landing on the moon.

"Too quiet."

From deep inside the crater they noticed a movement.

"Stand back, don't go in there, it's . . . it's . . . it's . . ."

"Moon Mummy!" they yelled together as two gray hands grabbed them from behind.

Now that was writing. Those were the good old creative days.

"Er . . . Booker," Germ said. "I forgot to tell you."

"Tell me what?" Booker asked as he accepted the pink slip with two fingers, as if it were composed of a toxic substance.

"I made an appointment for you with the Ox."

"His name is Mr. Oxford," Mr. Filippone said mildly.

Booker narrowed his eyes at Germ. "You didn't. You couldn't. You wouldn't."

"I had to. We need to get permission to give the speech."

"You told me it was all arranged."

"It almost is, Booker. I know he'll say yes to you. He likes you. He hates me."

"But if I don't get permission . . ."

"You will."

"I won't—he hates me too. Remember?" Booker

made one of the faces he had made that day in the hall.

"Boys?" Mr. Filippone raised his eyebrows. "Wherever you are going, go."

Booker didn't answer. He passed by Mr. Filippone and walked quickly toward Mr. Oxford's office. Booker Jones, person, now had to go and try to get permission to give a speech that he was incapable of writing.

11

<u>Moi?</u>

"I just don't see how you could be having trouble in school!" His mother held his chapter test. "You've always made good grades."

They looked at each other over the small plastic plates of their Lean Cuisines. He had waited until after dinner to break the news.

"I'm not exactly having trouble," Booker said. "I just can't get long division."

"It's the same thing," his mother said. She rubbed her eyes with both hands. "I just—"

Libba twirled into the kitchen.

"We say *Wolf Pack!*

"You say *aaooooooo!*

"*Wolf Pack, aaooooooo! Wolf Pack, aaooooooo!*"

Libba danced around waving her pompoms. She swung to the left and shook them. She swung them to the right. She put them on top of Booker's head and wiggled them. "Yeaaaahhhh! Wolf Pack!"

"Quit it!" he said irritably, engulfed in the burgundy and gold plastic strings.

"Libba! Stop that!" his mother said.

"Our squad's leading the cheers before the PTO meeting tomorrow," said Libba. "I've got to practice."

"Practice somewhere else," she said.

"Mo-om," she whined. "There *is* nowhere else." She propped one leg up on the countertop. "I need room to do my heel stretches."

"There's your *room*," Booker said.

"Speaking of my room," said Libba. "Mom, didn't I tell you Booker was in bothering my stuff Saturday?"

His mother slapped the test paper down onto the table. "I just can't take one more thing. Not one more. Pop is sick, and I am no nurse. I can't stand to be around sick people. When you kids were sick your father had to look after you. I'm not proud of it. I just can't stand to be around sick people." Her voice was loud and strained. "I was thinking this morning that I wish I could go back to the bank—the bank!"

Booker and Libba didn't move. Their mother's face was very pale.

"Look at this." She tipped her head down. "Gray hair."

"I don't see any gray hair, Mom," Booker said. "Well, one."

Their mother seemed to give herself a little shake. "Libba, get that leg off the counter and come over here. You are just going to help your brother with his long division. I cannot do one more thing!"

76

"Moi?" Libba looked at Booker in surprise.

Booker felt a glimmer of satisfaction at her distress, until he realized that it was at his expense.

"Moi? Help dweeb brain?"

"Yes. Help *your brother.*"

"Mom, she doesn't have to help me," Booker tried. "Mr. Filippone said he would help me."

"Well, we'll just get a head start right now. Libba, sit down. Booker, get your book."

He stared at Libba. She stared back.

"Mom, Germ could help me. I could go to Germ's house."

His mother's nostrils flared. "I seem to recall that Germ Germondo is not even in your math group."

"Okay, okay," he said. "I'll get my book."

When he returned to the kitchen Libba was sitting at the table, her pompoms resting next to the salt and pepper shakers.

They glared at each other for a moment.

Booker's mother was clearing the dishes off the table. She stopped and sat down beside him. "I'm sorry I lost my temper, kids. I know things have been hard for you, too. Booker, you don't even have anywhere to do your homework." She rested her head in her hands.

"I don't know what to do about Pop," she went on. "He doesn't show any signs of recovering. I don't know how long I can go on taking care of him if he doesn't begin to get better. And retirement homes won't even consider anyone who can't walk in under their own steam."

"What about Happy Homes?" Libba said. "That always sounded nice to me."

"They all *sound* nice," their mother replied wearily.

"Well, not Pickle Springs Retirement Home."

Their mother nodded. "I went to look at it last week and all the old people were lined up in the hall, and as I walked by they reached out to me. One man said, 'Take me home.' It almost broke my heart. I couldn't put my father in a place like that."

"What about Plantation Gardens?"

"That would be the best. But we can't afford it."

She looked at them. Booker had the feeling that some response was required, but he didn't know what to say.

"Anyway," she sighed. "This is not anything for you two to be worried about. You worry about long division. I'm just sorry I lost my temper."

Booker watched his mother stand up and carry the last few dishes to the sink.

Libba blinked, then picked up his book and read aloud: " 'Take the dividend and the divisor' . . . This is so bo-ring." She slammed the book shut and put it down. "Long division is easy," she said, standing up. "That book just makes it hard. Long division has four steps. You do the same four steps over and over. You just have to remember them. Think of it like this."

She picked up her pompoms. "One two three," she yelled. His mother, who was standing at the counter preparing Pop's tray, looked up and frowned.

"Divide!" Libba twirled the pompoms to one side with a swish.

"Multiply!" She stooped down low and gave the pompoms another swish.

"Subtract!" She brought the pompoms up, shaking them on the way.

"Bring down!" She finished with a jump, then stood with arms akimbo. "Remember those steps and you have it," she said. "You just do them over and over."

Booker's mother's frown had changed to a smile. She laughed and clapped. Booker smiled. He hadn't heard his mother laugh in what seemed like a long time.

"You try it." Libba handed the pompoms to Booker.

"No pompoms," he said.

"Come on," Libba insisted. "It will help you remember it better."

"Try it, Booker," his mother encouraged. "What can it hurt?" She smiled again and he felt his resistance crumble.

He stood up and took the pompoms, then glanced nervously toward the window, hoping that no one would happen to walk by and see him doing the cheers.

"One two three," Libba yelled. Then she pointed at him in a "take it away" gesture.

"Divide!" he said. He stuck one foot out awkwardly.

"Multiply!" He hit himself once with the pompoms, then got them to the other side. He was getting into the feeling of it.

"Subtract!" He kicked out a foot and accidentally knocked over a chair.

"Bring down!" he yelled.

His mother was laughing and wiping her eyes with a dish towel.

"Again!" his mother and Libba called together.

"You have great timing," Libba said, "but add more spirit."

"One two three," he yelled, hands on hips.

"Divide! Uh huh," he added.

He twirled the pompoms.

"Multiply! Uh huh!

"Subtract!" He twirled all the way around this time.

His mother leaned against the counter, laughing even harder.

"Bring down! Yeah!" he added as he shook the pompoms over his head, and in a moment of inspiration, tried one of Libba's toe jumps.

At that moment he saw Germ's face, wide-eyed, staring in through the picture window.

Great timing, all right.

12

Levitate!

"Man," said Germ. "I wish I hadn't seen that."

Germ and Booker were sitting on the front steps of the house. The air was cool and the sky was clear.

"My mom made me do it," said Booker. "They're trying to teach me how to do long division."

"Family." Germ gave him a sympathetic look, then added, "So what do you think?" He had what looked like a mud pie on his head.

"I think someone barfed on your head," Booker answered. "What is it?"

"My wolf hat. It's part of the costume. It adds five inches to my height."

"How did you make it?"

"Papier-mâché. I formed it over an old baseball hat. See?" He took it off and turned it over. "So, what did Ox say?"

"I don't think you deserve to know."

"Come on," Germ pleaded. "Please?"

"I still can't believe you did that—you actually made an appointment for me with Mr. Oxford."

"I apologize, okay? I'm sorry. I beg your forgiveness." Germ got down on his knees. "Now, just tell me."

If he did tell Germ, Germ would think that he made up the whole story.

"Fact or fiction?" he could imagine Germ asking. It had definitely been more like fiction.

"Yes, Booker?" Mr. Oxford had asked in his Darth Vader voice. "You needed to see me?"

Booker had sat on the edge of the large wooden chair in front of Mr. Oxford's desk. He noticed that Mr. Oxford had a miniature guillotine next to his stapler.

"We were wondering . . . I was wondering . . . Well, most of us were wondering . . ."

Mr. Oxford sat back and stared at Booker.

"It's about the Wolf Pack."

Mr. Oxford rolled his eyes. "Oh, that," he said. "My hands are tied. The PTO is going to vote on it. The school board always agrees with whatever they decide. If it passes, we'll be the Pickles."

"We want to have a rally before the meeting," Booker heard himself saying. "The kids want to come."

Mr. Oxford looked hard at Booker. He pressed his lips together tightly. Then he smiled. "Fine."

"Fine?"

"Yes. Fine."

"Can we give speeches?"

"Sure."

Booker's mouth had a difficult time staying closed.

"Yes, you can make a speech. Make it good, Booker. Make it great."

Mr. Oxford seemed to catch himself. He settled back into his seat. "Will that be all?" the Darth Vader voice asked.

Booker nodded and rose to leave.

"Booker?"

He turned at the door.

"One more thing."

"Yes."

Mr. Oxford lifted his head and howled. *"Aaaoooooooooo!"*

Booker realized the mistake he had made with the Moon Mummy character. The Moon Mummy always did the same things. Booker had just learned that a character should always be a little unpredictable.

"Booker." Germ inched forward on his knees, his hands clasped. "Puh-lease tell me. What did the Ox say? Can you give the speech or not?"

Booker's stomach tightened at the word *speech*. "Yeah," he said.

"Yes!" Germ said. "I knew he would let you. Have you got it written? I want to hear you. You'll need to practice. That's why I came over—to find out what Ox said and then to be your audience."

"I'm not quite ready for an audience."

"But you've got to give it tomorrow. The students

of Pickle Springs Middle School are counting on you. *I* am counting on you."

Booker's hands started to sweat. He wiped them on his T-shirt. "Why don't you do it?" he said. "You like to talk. You would be better at giving it than me."

"I don't deny that. But I have my own job. I am going to introduce you. And besides, you are the one who has Ox's permission."

"Why don't you write it?"

"No way," said Germ. "I couldn't even write one pickle joke. Remember, I'm the one who got a D in Creative Writing. I think Mrs. Doster has something against me."

"Maybe it's your writing," said Booker.

"Hey, like that last assignment? She said to write a beginning, middle, and end, and I did."

"Yeah, but it was only three sentences long."

"So? I did the assignment, didn't I?"

"Like the time she said to write something and you wrote the word *something*?"

"She didn't like that one either. You're not chickening out, are you?"

"No."

"I mean, you better not chicken out. It wasn't easy to get that appointment with Ox. I did my part."

"I know," said Booker. "I gotta go work on it."

"Make it good. Every kid in school will be there. The high-school kids are coming too. Even the elementary-school kids. You'll give your speech right at the end. The exciting climax."

Booker's stomach was so tight now that he thought if he opened his mouth it would spring out like the rubber bands he used to wind up his balsa-wood airplanes.

"We're going to be great," Germ continued. "We'll sway the crowd with moving words. We'll bring the mob to tears. You *will* write in some sad parts, won't you?"

Booker stood up. He couldn't bear to discuss the speech any longer.

"You listening? Make some sad parts."

"I gotta go," Booker said. "I need to take a shower." He almost added, *With a yellow legal pad and a Ticonderoga No. 2 pencil.*

"Okay," Germ said. "See you at the bus tomorrow." He picked up his bike from where he'd propped it against the steps. "Wolf Pack forever! *Aaooooooo!*" he called over his shoulder as he rode away.

Booker sat back down on the steps. The lights were on inside the house, but he didn't want to go in. When he went in it would be . . . He couldn't find the right word. *Stifling? Congested?*

Outside, the air was clear and there was space. He felt the rubber band unwind a little. He sat very still. Being by himself. Being himself—or trying to be.

He *wanted* to be himself, but suddenly he realized that he didn't know who he was anymore. He knew who he used to be. He had been defined clearly just by his room. The neat shelves of books said *reader.* The piles of journals said *writer.* The A's on his school papers said *good student.*

But lately everything had changed. He put his head on his arms and looked at the stars. They were clearly visible tonight. A single star shot across the sky. "Space cows," he murmured. He could see them in his mind, gliding above him, searching for intelligence.

His characters were so clear in his mind. To think that one week ago they had not even existed and now they seemed real. It was as if somewhere in the sky, in outer space, they really existed. Gliding through meteor showers, avoiding black holes, fighting the pig aliens.

He thought about the captain, strong and handsome and in control.

Bovinia was kind and funny.

Angus was goofy but nice.

Your characters come from yourself, he had read one time. Was it true even with space cows?

Was he in control, kind and funny, goofy but nice? He used to be. He reached up his hands, as if the space cows could swoop down and carry him off with them.

"Levitate!" he called to no one.

He would not have been one bit surprised if a beam of light had shot down from the sky and lifted him up and away into the cowship. He could go with them and leave his own battles—his own stories—behind. *The Attack of Sistoid. My Father the Coffee Cup. The Boy in the Black Hole.*

"Levitate!" he called one more time, just because it felt good to say it. He smiled. For a second he seemed to find a little bit of his old self.

"Booker," Libba called through the screen door. "Levitate *yourself* and get in here! It's your turn to load the dishwasher. Mo-om, Booker's hiding outside so he won't have to do the dishes!"

The image of his old self disintegrated and he was dweeb brain again. Booker opened the door and went inside the stifling, congested house.

13

His Life as a Book

"Booker! Get up!" His mother knocked on top of the dining room table. Before Booker even opened his eyes, an invisible hand squeezed his heart, and he woke up breathing too fast. The day of the rally had arrived, and he was speechless.

If his life were a book, he would set the scene with weather. The sky would be dark, with menacing black clouds. He would have thunder rumbling in the distance.

He crawled out from under the table and looked out the window. Remarkably, there was clear blue sky.

If his life were a book, this would be the part where he would write the words, *The time has come*.

"I'm out of clean underwear," Libba called from her room.

Booker walked down the hall toward the bathroom, feeling more alone than he ever had. On the worst day of his life, facing the most terrible problem of his twelve years on earth, he had no one to help him.

"Oh no you don't." Libba slipped into the bathroom ahead of him. "You are not going to take another marathon shower while I wait." The door closed in his face.

"Forget the makeup," he called. "It won't help." He pounded halfheartedly a few times on the door, then noticed a glow of yellow light coming from his old bedroom. He stopped pounding and moved toward the light until he stood in the doorway, pausing for a minute to look around the room.

It was dim except for the small reading light beside the bed. His mother had stopped opening the blinds. Around the room his things looked strangely out of place. He had not realized that he had so many books. And his posters seemed childish—the Braves looked odd on the wall. A mobile that he had made of his favorite book jackets hung pathetically out of balance from the ceiling. Piles of laundry were stacked in the corner. Dirty glasses were everywhere.

It reminded him of the picture games that they used to work in kindergarten. "Circle the things that do not belong." There would be a picture of the woods and you would circle a clock in a tree or a fish in a bird's nest. Here in his room, his things seemed out of place. He glanced longingly at his desk, where dirty clothes filled the chair, and then looked at his grandfather. "Pop?" he said.

Pop's eyes were open. He was awake.

It struck Booker how much he missed Pop—the old Pop. The old Pop would be the one now who could help him. He could have given Booker the authorly advice that he needed about his speech. He would have taken the time to listen and to help him figure out how to solve the problem.

On the top shelf of his bookcase Booker spotted his green notebook of Pop's columns. He walked across the room and pulled it from the shelf, then dumped the dirty clothes out of the desk chair and pulled it up to the bed. He sat down and held the notebook in his lap.

"Pop," he said, "this is the worst day of my life."

There was no reply.

"Did you ever have a time when you had a deadline and you couldn't write? I mean couldn't write anything? Nothing? Nada? Zilch?"

Pop didn't answer but his eyes focused on Booker—two bright beads.

"I have that problem now." Booker rambled on, not caring anymore if he was understood. It felt good for a moment to have someone to talk to even if he wasn't talking back.

"And Pop, I'm in trouble, because once people think you're a writer they expect more of you. And sometimes you can't give it. Like they expect me to be able to write a speech. A good speech. A good speech . . . *today*."

Pop blinked.

"I used to be a writer and now I'm just a plain person."

He heard the bathroom door open and close. "Your turn, dweeb brain," Libba called.

"I used to be a person, and now I'm a dweeb brain." Booker stood. He paused a moment, waiting to see if Pop would answer, but he lay frail and quiet on the bed.

"Bye, Pop," he said. He walked to the door and looked back, and saw that Pop had followed him with his eyes. "Thanks for listening."

As he got ready for school Booker wondered how long it would be before things were back to normal. Pop would be back at the river, fishing and writing, and he would be back in his own room at last.

"Come get some breakfast, Booker!" his mother called.

When he walked into the kitchen, he noticed that something was missing. He could almost hear his old first-grade teacher's cheerful voice saying, "Who notices something different today?"

His father's coffee cup was gone.

"Where's Dad?" he said.

"What do you mean?" His mother looked up from a stack of Pop's insurance forms on the table.

"His coffee cup's not here."

"He left late last night to ride up to the Write House. He's showing the place to some people today," she said. "They have a bait shop out near the river and they might be able to rent out the place to fishermen for us."

"Pop's not going back." Booker said it as a statement, not a question. The idea took him by surprise, yet how could he have failed to notice the signs? The boxes for one thing. Would his parents have moved all Pop's things here if he could ever go back? They had known it all along.

His mother brushed back a stray lock of hair. "No," she said quietly, as if she was telling herself as well as Booker. "Pop's not going back. His hip has healed but he still is not getting better. He should be getting up and around by this time. When I think of him up at the river alone . . ." She shook her head. "It's too dangerous to let him go back."

"But the retirement homes?"

She shook her head again. "It just won't work, Booker."

He had been waiting for the moment when everything would get back to normal. When Pop would be back at the river, fishing and writing columns. When he would be back in his room with his bookshelves and desk. When his brain would be uncluttered and free again to write. Now he realized that that was never going to happen, and there was nothing he could do about it.

Booker wondered if they had told Pop yet that he wasn't going back to live at the river. He wouldn't be happy. Would he even understand? Like Booker, he wasn't in control of his life.

If Booker's life were a book, his fate would be dictated by the words of the story, and he knew from his extensive reading that the worst always happens in books.

If a boy is flying in an airplane across the Canadian wilderness, the plane goes down.

If a boy is on a Dutch freighter during a war, with enemy submarines around, the ship is going to sink.

If a boy's grandfather falls and breaks his hip, he does not get better. If a boy is headed toward a rally with thousands of people waiting to hear a speech that the boy has not written . . . The possibilities were too awful to consider.

He had lost his faith in happy endings.

14

Place Value

"Place value." Mr. Filippone was tapping the chalkboard with his stick. Booker held his green notebook behind Haines Wilson and thumbed through the yellowed newspaper clippings. He read Pop's words, hoping to find an answer to his problem—any answer.

> *It's an ordinary place. My river.*
>
> *I wake to the call of geese, each voice a happy note of optimism. I wake to the smell of pine needles and fresh clear air. I sit in my lawn chair and look out at my little stretch of water, so ordinary, flowing past my cottage. Ordinary currents of clear green water, over ordinary rocks. Ordinary sunbeams reflecting on ordinary ripples. An endless stream of water that has passed this land for hundreds of years. It was here long before I came. It will be here long after I'm gone. My ordinary river.*

Booker felt his chest tighten as he read Pop's words of love for the river. To Pop, the river was not an ordinary place at all.

"Place value," Mr. Filippone said even louder. He tapped harder on the board. Booker did not even look up. He was drawn to Pop's words.

"Class, are you with me?"

Booker turned the pages. He ran his finger across his grandfather's name at the top of the column: Judd Harrison. This was the grandfather that he remembered.

"Okay, class. I give up." Mr. Filippone stood with his hands raised in a gesture of resignation. "Put your math books away. I know tonight is the PTO meeting. How many of you are going?"

Every hand went up.

"I'm proud of you all. You care about something and you're doing something about it. Let's all take out a sheet of paper."

There was a shuffling as everyone complied.

"Write these words: *Dear Mr. Oxford.*"

Germ waved his hand in the air. "Why? Why would we write that?"

"Hold on, Germ. We're going to write letters about the Wolf Pack. We'll start with our principal."

"Nothing like starting at the bottom."

"I didn't hear that," Mr. Filippone said.

Catherine Cowan raised her hand. "Can you start us out?" she asked.

"Let's see ... Write, *Dear Mr. Oxford, we do not want to be the Pickles because* ... You take it from there."

Booker didn't write. He had found an amazing column—one that he had not remembered. It was about his grandmother. She had died before Booker was born.

I don't miss her much. Her yarn and knitting nee-dles still wait beside her favorite chair—the red sweater half done. I think I'll keep them there for a while.

I don't miss her much. Her flowered hat still hangs on the hook by the back door. I think I'll keep it too.

Booker closed the notebook. He couldn't read any more. He had seen that hat among Pop's belongings piled against the wall in the dining room. He had been so busy worrying about his own problems that he had stopped thinking of Pop. Pop had lost far more than he had.

For once, while everyone else in the room was writing, he was thinking not about fiction but about fact and reality. And it came to him: one thing, one small thing, that he could do.

The bell rang. Booker sat still, staring at the cover of the notebook.

"Earth to Booker." Mr. Filippone tapped him gently on the head with the stick. Booker looked up. "You okay?"

Booker nodded. He stood and tucked the green leather notebook under his arm. "Just thinking," he said.

"About math, I hope?"

"No, just about something I have to do."

"Well," said Mr. Filippone, "do it."

15

Changing Places

"Pop?"

No answer. Pop still stared at the ceiling, his hands folded across his chest. The blinds were closed, the room dark. The medicine smell wafted out at Booker.

He went swiftly into the dining room, where he looked at the boxes lining the walls. He picked up one of the boxes and carried it to his old room.

"Look, Pop," he said. Pop blinked but didn't answer. "Here's your stuff." He nodded at the picture of the fish staring from the frame on top of the box.

Pop slowly raised his head and stared at the box blankly for a moment. Then his head dropped back against the pillows and his eyes turned back to the ceiling.

Booker set the box down with a plop. He pulled out the first picture and dusted it off with the end of the bedspread. He took down his Braves poster and hung up the picture of the staring fish.

He took the spaceship models down from his shelf

and put them on the floor. Then he wiped the dusty shelf with the edge of his T-shirt, and one by one put the collection of framed pictures from the box onto the newly clean shelf.

After another trip to the dining room, Pop's flannel shirts and overalls replaced his T-shirts and jeans in the bureau.

A load of hip boots and waders soon replaced the tennis shoes on his closet floor.

Rods and reels replaced his collection of books.

Libba came and stood at the door and watched him work. Booker waited for a comment but none came. She disappeared, returning with a bottle of Windex and some rags. She began to clean off the shelves where Booker had removed his things. She dusted each picture frame and put it back in place.

Pop watched them silently as they worked. Booker gathered up the dirty glasses from the nightstand and took them to the kitchen.

Together Booker and Libba gathered the piles of dirty towels and sheets and took them to the laundry room and brought two more boxes from the dining room.

From one box Booker unfolded a large brown-and-gold afghan and put it on the bed in place of his old bedspread. From the other box Libba took out their grandmother's straw hat and hung it on the back of Booker's chair. They packed Booker's things into the empty boxes.

Back and forth they went from the dining room to the bedroom until every trace of his old room was gone.

It did not look like a boy's room anymore, it looked like Pop's room. Booker turned the pole on the blinds and light filtered through. He opened the window and a breeze blew in.

"Pop," Booker said finally when everything was done, "this is your room now."

Pop didn't answer but his hands moved along the familiar edge of the brown-and-gold afghan. Then he closed his eyes and slept.

When Booker finally crawled under the dining room table, exhausted, there was his typewriter. Libba had given it back.

Sometimes Libba did something so nice so unexpectedly that it made his head spin. He remembered when he had forgotten his lunch on the first day of middle school. He didn't even know how to buy lunch, and he didn't have any money. He had spent all morning worrying about lunch. When he had gone to his locker between periods to change his books, there was Libba with his lunch. He had been so overjoyed to see that brown paper bag that he had almost kneeled down and said a prayer of thanks in the middle of the Pickle Springs Middle School hall.

Booker touched the top of the typewriter gently. He looked at the pile of white typing paper beside the typewriter, but he had no desire to put a sheet in and type.

It was quiet now. He was alone, surrounded not by Pop's boxes but by his own. He didn't know how long he had stayed under the table, when two blue slippers appeared. "Booker?" his mother's voice called. He stuck his head out and pulled back the sheet so that she could come in.

His mother crawled under the sheet and sat cross-legged on one end of the sleeping bag.

"Thanks for helping Pop."

"It's nothing, Mom."

"It is *not* nothing. Thank you, Booker." She smiled a little, then sighed. "I keep waiting for Pop to get better. I forget that he's ninety-two years old."

"Will he ever get better, Mom?"

"He might, Booker. But he might not."

"Is he still Pop?" It was a funny question to ask, but she seemed to understand.

"Yes." His mother was quiet for a minute. "When you and Libba were babies—you can't imagine how much I loved you."

Booker remembered the resplendent faces of his parents in his baby picture. He nodded.

"You couldn't talk or walk or communicate at all except by crying. It didn't matter, you were still my children. That's how I feel about Pop. He's still Pop whether he talks again or walks again—he'll still be my father."

"And my grandfather," Booker added.

"That's right," his mother said. "I'm proud of you and your sister and the way you two have been helping out. I think I can do it, Booker. I mean, I think I can keep Pop here. If you and Libba and Dad help."

"We'll help," Booker said.

"Your father and I are going to try to do something in here for you. Put up some doors . . ."

"It doesn't matter, Mom," Booker said, and he meant it.

At last the something that was crowding his head was gone; for the first time since Pop moved in he had a sense of peace. He felt more like himself than he had in a long while.

"Anyway." His mother began crawling out from underneath the table. "It's time for the rally. Libba's gone with Alyse, and she forgot her rally rag. Can you take it when you go?"

"Sure." Booker eased out from under the table and took the brown square of cloth that his mother held out.

"You need a ride?"

"No, I'll walk." He was in no hurry to get there. He had gone all day without thinking of his speech, and now it was too late.

As he walked to school, he could hear the band playing in the distance. He could hear people cheering.

So his name would never be in the book of great speeches. So he would never join the ranks of the great speech writers: Abe Lincoln, General Patton, John F. Kennedy. It didn't bother him so much. At least he had peace.

Suddenly, in the midst of the peace, he had the glimmer of an idea for his speech. He stopped in the middle of the sidewalk and tried to concentrate. A small idea, but an idea. How could he have not thought of it before! He looked around and felt in his pockets. He had a pen but he had nothing to write on—no typewriter, no yellow legal pads, not even the back of an envelope.

Then Booker remembered a story he'd read about Roald Dahl. Dahl had been driving down a road in his car when he got the idea for a book about an elevator. He pulled over to the side of the road and wrote with his finger on the dirty rear window of the car the word *elevator*.

If Roald Dahl could write on a window, then he, Booker, could find *something* to write on. He looked at the rally rag and grinned. He couldn't. He shouldn't. He could and he would. He sat down on the curb and began to write. This would be the best speech in the history of the United States. The world? The universe?

If his life were a book, this was the moment when he would look up and see sunshine peeking out from behind a dark cloud. Booker checked the sky. It was blue. On the horizon though was one tiny gray cloud, gilded with a ray of sunlight.

16

Rally!

"Wolf Pack! Wolf Pack! *Aaaooooooooo!*"

Booker ran down the sidewalk toward the sound of the cheers, his finished speech clutched in his hand. The closer he got to the school the louder the voices became until he turned the last corner and saw the rally in full swing.

Hundreds of kids yelled and waved brown rally rags in front of the school. The cheerleaders led the chants and the pep band played a fight song in the background as a large group of parents and teachers stood and watched. Booker could see Libba twirling her pompoms. She didn't seem worried about her rally rag.

He stopped at the edge of the crowd to catch his breath and looked around frantically for Germ. Finally he spotted him, wearing his wolf hat and standing at the top of the stairs to the platform that Mr. Oxford used when he addressed assemblies. The brown podium was decorated with ribbons and a large WPKL sign from the radio station, and two large black speakers stood on either side of it. Booker's stomach tightened as he realized the radio station was broadcasting the rally. "Germ!" he yelled, but the sound of his voice was lost in the noise of the crowd. Germ was gazing out over the crowd, probably looking for Booker.

Booker pushed his way among the kids, waving, until Germ saw him and motioned for him to come up the stairs. "You got it?" Germ asked anxiously, a trickle of brown sweat rolling down his temple. "I was afraid you weren't coming. It's almost over and they're ready for us. Have you got the speech?"

Booker nodded.

With a sigh of relief Germ grabbed his arm and pulled him toward the podium. "He's here!" Germ called to a man in a WPKL T-shirt at the microphone. "We're ready!"

The man nodded and began to wave his arms to quiet the crowd.

"So, where is it?" Germ asked.

Booker held up the rally rag.

"That's it?" Germ's voice went up two notes.

"Trust me," Booker said. "It's a great speech."

"You're kidding, right?"

"No joke. It's the best speech in the United States. The world. The universe."

Germ looked at the brown cloth and grabbed his throat.

The crowd was still chanting. "Wolf Pack! Wolf Pack! *Aaoooooo!*"

The man in the WPKL T-shirt waved his hands in wider arcs to get their attention, until finally the crowd quieted. "Now we have a word from a Pickle Springs Middle School student, Germ Germondo, who will introduce our speaker." He gestured for Germ to come to the mike.

Germ didn't move.

"Germ?" Booker nudged Germ forward, and he staggered to the microphone. Drops of perspiration were rolling down the sides of his face. He opened his mouth, but no sound came out. For the first time in his life Germ was speechless.

"Germ, say something," Booker whispered urgently. Germ opened his mouth and tried again. This time a noise like a sick elephant came from somewhere inside him.

The man from the radio station gently moved Germ aside. "I believe that we will now hear a speech from"—he glanced at a note in his hand—"Booker Jones, who will talk about the Wolf Pack."

"*Aaooooooo!*" people yelled.

Booker clutched the rally rag as he moved forward to the microphone, which whined a little as he bumped against it. What seemed like hundreds of faces were looking up at him, waiting expectantly for his speech. Booker looked out at the sea of faces and blinked.

The rally rag trembled a little in his hand. He smoothed it out onto the podium and began in his most serious voice.

"Parents, teachers, and fellow students of Pickle Springs Middle School: We come today to make a decision. Shall it be pickles?"

"Boooo!" the crowd responded.

"Or wolves?"

"*Aaooooooo!*"

"The PTO wants to change us to the Pickles because they say that it's unfair to wolves for them to be our mascot. I come before you today, after careful thought, to ask you, honorable parents and teachers, to vote *for* the Fighting Pickles."

He could hear a hostile murmur run through the crowd.

"Hear me out! Wolves are not the only animals that deserve our respect. I propose a few additional changes, out of respect for our other four-legged friends.

"Coach Buzbee shall no longer be called Buzbee. His name is much too insulting to bees. He will hereafter be known as Coach Buzpickle."

Booker paused and looked out at the audience with his most solemn expression and saw ... smiles. They were smiling at him. It was working. At least they knew he wasn't serious about voting for the fighting pickles. But ... were they laughing *at* him or *with* him? He looked at his shaking hands and tried to will them to be still.

"And Mrs. Bullock, our art teacher, will now be called Mrs. Pickle-ock out of respect for the bulls of the world."

There was a ripple of laughter in the crowd.

Libba was hiding her face in her pompoms. Booker could feel a drop of sweat running down his forehead. Maybe he should have gone for a more serious speech. Had they laughed at Churchill? Had they laughed at Patrick Henry?

"Go on," whispered Germ in a cracked voice. "Go on."

"Catherine Cowan shall be Catherine Pickle-an.

"Jon Birdsong will change to Jon Picklesong.

"Germ Germondo shall be Pickle Picklemondo. We wouldn't want the germs to be offended.

"Cara Newton shall be Cara Pickle-on out of respect for newts."

A woman was dabbing her eyes with a tissue. A man was bent over laughing. Booker read on faster. The faster he read the faster it would be over.

"And finally, our dear and respected principal, Mr. Oxford . . ."

He paused and took a breath. He could see Mr. Oxford off to the side of the crowd bouncing up and down on the balls of his feet.

". . . will from now on be Mr. Pickleford, out of respect to our four-legged oxen friends. Why not replace these names, out of concern for oxen and bees and newts and germs . . ."

He paused again.

". . . and wolves? The time has come to listen to the voice of reason."

People were quiet now, and looked as if they were listening intently. Pop's technique had worked—Booker had their full attention. It was time to be serious. He gave them his most solemn presidential stare.

"What are names anyway? They are more than words. These words are our past . . ."

The crowd began to clap.

". . . our heritage . . ."

The crowd clapped louder.

". . . our history. Aren't these words our own identity?"

The roar of the crowd was deafening.

"Thank you, everyone."

Booker backed away from the microphone. He couldn't look out at the crowd anymore.

He was stirred by his own words. Words had the ability to do that—to actually make a person's heart beat faster, his breath quicken. He said a silent thank you to everyone who had ever used words to do that. Everyone from Pop to William Shakespeare.

The man from the radio station moved forward and spoke into the mike. "Let's hear it for Booker!" The applause continued as Booker and Germ made their way down the steps and into the crowd.

"I can't believe I did it," Booker said to Germ.

"They loved it!" Germ said, slapping him on the back.

"Booker Jones?" A man stepped up with a small notebook in his hands. "Did you write that speech yourself, son?" he asked.

Booker nodded.

"I'm Ross Johnson, a reporter for the *Pickle*

Springs Press, and we'd like to publish your speech in to-morrow's paper."

"You'd what?"

"We're doing an article about the rally and we want to include your speech. We'd like your permission to publish it."

"Publish?"

"Yes."

"Publish." Booker said the word once, then again. "Pub-lish?"

Mr. Johnson nodded. Booker shook out the rally rag and handed it to Mr. Johnson, who folded it carefully and put it in his pocket. "Look for it in tomorrow's paper," he said as he walked away.

Mr. Oxford was at the microphone now, announcing that the PTO vote would take place in the gymnasium. There was no doubt from the mood of the crowd how the vote would go. Parents were giving the wolf howl as they headed toward the gym.

"We did it!" Germ yelled. "We did it!"

Booker wasn't listening.

Pub-lish.

Germ was jumping up and down holding on to his arm but Booker was too shocked to move.

P-u-b-l-i-s-h.

It was amazing how one word could change your life.

As a writer, Booker always recognized the power of words. There was always the quest for the perfect word.

Mark Twain once said that the difference between the right word and the nearly right word is the same as that between lightning and the lightning bug.

Now Booker knew the power of words with an insight and clarity that he had not even imagined. A perfect word had changed his life. That word was the most beautiful word in the English language.

Publish.

17

By Booker Jones

"An author, a *published* author, needs to use the bath-room," Booker said, not bothering to pound on the door like he usually did. "You've been in there for forty-five minutes. I set my watch." The only reply was the sound of Libba's hair dryer.

"Forty-six!" he called out.

Booker rested his back against the wall. A smile came over his face as he thought about his article. For the first time in his life he had been waiting when the morning paper arrived. The delivery man left him five copies.

He looked down for about the hundredth time at the newspaper in his hand. His name in print was mag-nificent. His first byline.

Today a man named Mr. Garber and his son would be staying in the Write House for a week of fishing and jigsaw puzzles and roaring fires. They would be the first of many fishermen to enjoy the river.

Today his father was staying home to start building a wall and a door to close off the dining room, Booker's official new room. Later a new bed and dresser would be delivered from Bargain Buys to replace the dining room table.

"Forty-eight!" he called at the bathroom door, then gave up and headed down the hall. He stopped at Pop's door, realizing that he had not told Pop about his speech.

The light was on in Pop's room and something was different. Pop was sitting up today, resting back against the pillows. Booker couldn't tell for sure, but he thought Pop's face looked better, not so pale, less transparent.

"Hi, Pop." Booker sat down on the chair beside the bed. He smoothed the newspaper on his lap. Pop looked at him. "I did it. Remember the speech that I couldn't write? I wrote it." Booker held up the paper and pointed to it. He couldn't suppress the smile inside of himself.

"My speech, Pop. It's in the paper." He scooted the chair closer to the bed. "Here's my name, right here." He held the paper up for Pop to see. He pointed to his name.

"By Booker Jones. There's nothing like seeing your name in print, is there? You want to hear it?"

Booker stood up and cleared his throat. "Parents, teachers, fellow students," he began. As he read the speech he relived his moment of glory. He could almost hear the cheers.

"... Thank you, everyone." He ended with one arm extended, then clutched the paper to his chest. Instead of the applause of the crowd there was silence, but it was a satisfying silence. A companionable silence.

"Breakfast is ready," Booker's father called from the kitchen. "Come and get it!"

"I'll get your tray, Pop." Booker went to the door, then turned and paused. "And Pop. . . . Thanks."

Pop blinked.

"I mean, thanks for being here." Booker took another look at the room. Nothing was out of place. It looked just right.

"The author arrives!" his father said as Booker stopped in the kitchen doorway. Incredibly his father looked just the same. He stood at the stove turning pancakes. Bare feet, jeans, hair thinning at the top. Not at all cylindrical.

His mother and Libba sat at the kitchen table. They each had their own copy of the morning paper. As he walked into the kitchen his mother began to clap and Libba raised her arms in a victory sign with two invisible pompoms.

Booker was filled with a surprising sense of love for his family that he had not felt in a long time.

His life seemed to be coming back together like the jigsaw puzzles that they worked at the Write House. Pop's accident had been the motion that had shaken the pieces out. Now the pieces were falling into place again, but the picture on the puzzle had changed. And the new picture, he decided, though not perfect, was going to be all right. It was almost enough to make him believe in happy endings again.

The man grew larger, less cylindrical, less ceramic—back to himself. And the world was safe for coffee drinkers everywhere.

Sistoid broke from her shell, a dark-brown, scaly cocoon, and emerged in human form to bring kindness to the world.

The boy crawled slowly, torturously out of the black hole. Hand over hand he groped through the darkness until he saw a spot of light, brighter . . . brighter . . . brighter . . . and out! Out of the black hole.

Booker sat under the dining room table one last time. He hated to admit it but he was going to miss his tent. He adjusted his reading light and traced his fingers over the worn keys of the typewriter in a caress. He had known this old typewriter would write good books, great books. On it he could even write the best book in the history of the world—if only he could think of the last chapter.

He closed his eyes. He concentrated. Time for one more happy ending. The hum of the typewriter became the drone of the cowship. Booker Jones, person, stepped aside for a moment and Booker Jones, writer, took his place. It was time to send the space cows home. With a sigh of pure contentment he began to type.

The cowship grew smaller and smaller as it moved away from the planet called Earth—a comet of blazing light across the night sky, a glowing satellite moving away in the atmosphere, a tiny pinpoint of light in the darkness of space, then finally nothing.

Captain Jersey gazed one last time at the small planet in the distance. "Good-bye, Earth cows," he said to the emptiness of space. Then he repeated it in their own language. "Mooo." He turned to his companions. "We must leave now and return to our own planet."

"Forever?" Angus asked.

Captain Jersey watched the planet Earth as they moved away. "Nothing," he said as he switched the ship to warp speed, "is forever."

Booker Jones
Pickle Springs, AR

April 5

Hamerstein Books
New York, NY

Dear Editor:

    I did it! I did it! My novel. I finished
it! You will love it. Don't waste a minute.
Read the exciting climax and conclusion of ...
SPACE COWS!

Utterly yours,

Booker Jones
Published Author

Betsy Duffey is the author of numerous books for young readers, including *Coaster*; *The Gadget War*; *How to Be Cool in the Third Grade*; *Hey, New Kid!*; *The Math Wiz*; and the *Pet Patrol* series. She lives in Atlanta, Georgia.

Ellen Thompson has illustrated more than one hundred children's book jackets, and her work has appeared in numerous magazines. She lives in Franklin Park, New Jersey.